Interesting
Times

Matthew Storm

For Michele

"May you live in interesting times."

Chinese proverb

Chapter 1

Oliver Jones was 32 years old, single, and had always presumed that he lived one of the world's duller lives. He lived alone in a small house he rented in the quiet Sunset district of San Francisco. The house itself was an old Victorian that dated back to the 1960's and was completely unremarkable, even among the unremarkable row houses that were characteristic of this part of the city. He liked the neighborhood well enough, but it was never going to be on the front of a postcard.

Oliver worked as a financial analyst at Western Pacific Capital, a small, unremarkable hedge fund headquartered in the center of the city's financial district. Every weekday morning at exactly 7:04 a.m. he boarded the L train for the 45-minute ride to work. He usually spent the commute reading the newspaper or looking over spreadsheets he'd taken home the night before in order to get an early start on work, but that was mainly an excuse to avoid making eye contact with or speaking to other passengers. He didn't think of himself as being particularly anti-social, but San Francisco was a big city full of, as his mother had once warned him, colorful characters. Most people were harmless enough, but there were always the exceptions. One moment you were agreeing with someone that, yes, it did seem unusually foggy that morning, and the next you were realizing that particular comment hadn't been aimed at you at all, but rather to the invisible anthropomorphic rabbit sitting next to you. Oliver had decided some time ago that it was best to simply not bother in the first place. There were better places to meet people.

Oliver's job was in corporate research, which meant that he tried to get a fix on the financial health of different businesses. He did this by sifting through SEC filings, 10-K reports, earnings statements, and any other piece of paperwork a company might produce for the public to see. It was tedious work that he didn't particularly care for, but that he was generally acknowledged to be very good at. When he finished his analysis he would recommend to the firm's traders that they either buy, sell, or hold that particular company's stock. They were the ones who had the joy of actually doing something with the information he provided, while he moved on to his next analysis. Oliver was just a bit jealous of the traders, feeling that their jobs must be much more exciting than his own. If he'd had a few cocktails with people that didn't know any better, Oliver might imply that he himself was a trader, because he liked the idea that he did something more interesting at work than study spreadsheet columns all day. In fact, he did not.

After work Oliver would typically ride the train home, microwave something for dinner, and spend a few hours watching television. He didn't have many friends in the city so he spent most nights like this, alone. Weekends were not much different. More often than not he would go to the office for a few hours on Saturdays to get a jump on the next week's work.

It was not so much out of necessity, but because he really had nothing else to do.

All in all, he thought, it was a dull life. He didn't mind all that much, but on occasion he would find himself wishing for more. A little excitement. Adventure. Nothing crazy, though. He didn't fancy exotic vacations in South America or solo climbing up the side of a mountain with nothing but strong fingers and a bag of powdered chalk standing between him and a fall to his death. He just wanted a little something to get his adrenaline going.

Lately he had been thinking about getting a cat.

He already had a cat, in one sense. A stray tom had climbed onto his rear windowsill several months before, when Oliver had been keeping his back window open in a futile attempt to keep his house cool in the summer heat. Like most people in this part of the city, Oliver did not have central air conditioning. The cat had noticed Oliver eating and had meowed hopefully at him, and after a moment's consideration Oliver placed a piece of "grilled" teriyaki chicken from his microwave dinner onto the windowsill. The cat had downed the food enthusiastically and been a regular visitor ever since. Oliver wouldn't necessarily call him a pet, though. While he would permit some scratching behind his ears, the one time Oliver had tried to pick the cat up he had been hissed at angrily. Oliver hadn't tried again, although he had taken to calling the cat "Jeffrey" and found himself looking forward to his visits.

He was thinking about this while watching Jeffrey eat one evening. He had picked up take-out Chinese on his way home and was feeding the cat pieces of shrimp picked from his container of fried rice. The cat seemed to enjoy it much more than microwave food. Oliver wondered if he were to buy a litter box, would Jeffrey know how to use it? He had read somewhere that it was instinctive behavior with cats, once they knew where it was, but he wasn't so sure. Would the cat even come inside? He had never shown any interest in coming any farther than the windowsill, and Oliver was hesitant to try to pick him up again.

"Things would be easier if you could talk," he said to Jeffrey.

Oliver heard a strange sound in his ears, like rushing water coming up behind him. He felt suddenly dizzy, and the world seemed to begin to slide, spinning slowly around him, before equally suddenly snapping back into place.

Jeffrey glanced up at him, still chewing. "Nah, I doubt it," the cat said.

Oliver froze in place, his eyes wide. He saw the cat's own eyes widen in shock and his tiny mouth dropped open, little bits of shrimp tumbling down onto the windowsill.

"You...you talked!" Oliver stammered.

Jeffrey stared at Oliver. His head swung left and right as if trying to figure out where the new voice had come from, then he yowled in terror and darted away like a shot. Oliver watched as the cat easily scaled the wooden fence that surrounded his property, and then he was gone.

Oliver spent the better part of an hour puzzling over what had happened. The cat had talked, hadn't it? He had heard it as plainly as...well, anything. But of course he knew better. The only rational explanation was that the cat hadn't spoken at all. It could only have made one of the myriad sounds cats were capable of, and in his loneliness Oliver had hopefully imagined it was speech.

Or perhaps one of his neighbors had observed all of this through a gap in the fence, and also happened to be a skilled ventriloquist. Oliver would have had to admit that as unlikely as that scenario may have been, it made more sense than a cat speaking to him.

Oliver sighed deeply. If he were going to rank how pathetic this experience had been on a scale of one to ten, it probably came in at about a nine.

Preparing for bed later that night, Oliver wondered what he should do about it. Maybe getting a cat wasn't such a great idea. He clearly needed to spend more time with people and less talking to animals. This was probably how it started with cat ladies, he thought. You start talking to one cat, then to another, and the next thing you know you're eighty years old, living with twenty feline roommates in a house that constantly smelled of cat urine. He didn't want to end up that way.

Maybe he should take a class. He'd always liked cooking, even though he rarely did it anymore. A cooking class would be a good way to meet some people and also get him away from microwave dinners and take-out boxes. He could kill two birds with one stone.

That was definitely the way to go, he decided. There was a culinary school that held evening classes not terribly far from his office. He had seen their commercials on television. He could stop by there after work and see what they had to offer. He'd do it tomorrow.

And this time, he resolved, wasn't going to be like all the other times he had planned to do something and then never followed up on it. It was time to make a change in his life, and he was definitely going to make it this time.

And if a cat ever spoke to him again, he'd make an appointment with his doctor and get his head looked at.

Chapter 2

The next week passed without any further incidents. Jeffrey did not reappear at Oliver's windowsill and no other animals or objects spoke to him. What had happened with the cat seemed like a dream now. No doubt he had imagined the whole thing, and his startled reaction to that strange fantasy had scared the poor animal away. Oliver resolved to give the cat something special to eat if he ever returned. He recalled that Jeffrey had seemed to particularly enjoy the Thai food Oliver had brought home a few weeks before. Maybe he should order some and put a plate out on the windowsill where Jeffrey might smell it and come calling. Oliver had found he missed the little cat.

On a foggy Thursday morning a few days later Oliver found himself on a half-empty train on the way to his office. He had just remembered, for the tenth or eleventh time, that he had been meaning to sign up for a cooking class. He'd have to look into that tonight. Or maybe tomorrow. Yes, he'd definitely have time tomorrow.

The train stopped at 16th Avenue and three people boarded.

One of them stood out from the usual crowd of morning commuters. He was a tall, lanky man with bleached-blond hair, but what made him unique was his brightly colored Hawaiian shirt. Oliver was surprised. That shirt probably would have been considered a little over the top even in Waikiki, but in San Francisco it just looked ridiculous.

The man took a standing position a few feet away from Oliver as the train doors slid shut and the train began to move again. Oliver wondered if the man was a surfer. He looked like a surfer. Maybe he ought to take surfing lessons, Oliver thought. There were a few surf shops in the Sunset down near the beach. There must be a place there he could take lessons. He'd have to look into it. That *and* the cooking class. Tomorrow.

The train continued on as Oliver read his newspaper. There was trouble in the Middle East again. Had there ever *not* been trouble in the Middle East? In all of human history? He wasn't sure.

Oliver felt a tingling sensation on the back of his neck. Someone was watching him. He looked up quickly but the man in the Hawaiian shirt was reading something on his smartphone and nobody else was nearby. The man in the Hawaiian shirt glanced up to meet Oliver's gaze. "Nice day today," he said politely.

"Sure," said Oliver, going back to his newspaper.

"Going to be hot," the man said. Oliver nodded without thinking about it. The train was moving into the tunnel at West Portal station and would be in the city soon.

The rest of the commute was uneventful. Oliver got off the train at the last stop and walked two blocks to his building, an elegant high-rise on California Street. He worked on the 47th floor of a 48-story building. He liked it up there. His own office at the firm was small, but it had a large window with an expansive view. He could see all the way across the bay to Oakland and beyond.

Oliver spent his morning combing through a small tech company's annual 10-K report. There would be an earnings conference call in the afternoon and he wanted to prepare a few questions in advance. Each analyst on the call would be permitted only one question, but Oliver liked to have a few backups handy, just in case someone else asked a question too similar to his first choice before he had the chance.

Just before noon Oliver walked half a block to a small Mexican restaurant. This place could draw quite a lunch crowd and he liked to get in early to avoid a long wait. He was third in the take-out line when the door swung open behind him and the man in the Hawaiian shirt stepped inside. Oliver nearly did a double-take. This guy again? It had to be. Unless he had a twin with a similar terrible fashion sense.

The man in the Hawaiian shirt moved to stand directly behind Oliver and looked at the menu board curiously. "Oh, you were on my train," he said to Oliver. "Hello again."

"Hello," Oliver nodded.

"Good food here?" the man asked. "I've never been."

"Sure," said Oliver, feeling a bit confused. What were the odds of this? After some thought, he had to admit that the odds were pretty good, actually. San Francisco didn't have a huge number of tourist destinations and several of the major ones were nearby. Union Square and the Ferry Building were within easy walking distance. The cable cars ran through this area, and Fisherman's Wharf would only be a fifteen-minute ride away. The man in the Hawaiian shirt was obviously a tourist, given his attire. He was probably just out seeing the sights.

"I love Mexican food," the man told him.

"Oh. Well, the burritos are good here," said Oliver.

"Oh, yeah? Thanks, buddy," the man smiled.

Oliver left the restaurant with a shrimp burrito in a small plastic bag. San Francisco had banned plastic bags from grocery stores some time ago, he remembered. Had that applied to restaurants as well? He wasn't sure.

The fog hadn't lifted and it was starting to get windy. Oliver wished he'd brought his jacket along. It had been overcast all day and now the sky was threatening to rain.

Hadn't the man in the Hawaiian shirt said it was going to be hot, back on the train? Oliver frowned. It hadn't occurred to him at the time, but rain had been in the forecast for several days. It hadn't been hot in the city for weeks. What an odd thing to have said. Oliver pondered it for a moment. So the man had been wrong. Fair enough. He was a tourist and was probably unfamiliar with the weather here. But what a silly thing to be wrong about, especially when he had just been standing outside waiting for a train. Even once on board, all you had to do to check the weather was look through the window.

Back in his firm's 47th floor lobby, Oliver noticed a visitor sitting in the waiting area. The man wore a black suit with a fierce-looking red tie and had a stern demeanor Oliver had seen in other men before. He was probably a process server, or some kind of federal inspector. Everything about him said "official business," and probably unpleasant business at that. Someone at his firm was about to have a very bad day. He felt sorry for whoever *that* was.

Donna, the firm's receptionist, was a cheerful redhead in her mid-forties. Oliver had never seen her without a smile, but now she was biting her bottom lip nervously. "Mr. Jones?" she asked, just as he was about to pass by.

Oliver frowned. Donna always called him by his first name. "What is it, Donna?"

She looked toward the waiting area. "There's someone here to see…"

"Oliver Jones?" Oliver turned to see the man in the black suit had risen and was now standing directly in front of him, close enough the Oliver could feel the man's cool breath on his face. He took a short step back as the man held up his identification. "Hilary Teasdale. Securities and Exchange Commission."

"Hello," Oliver said. He extended his hand, which Mr. Teasdale shook pleasantly. The other man's skin was dry and smooth and felt oddly thin, like paper.

"A pleasure to meet you," Mr. Teasdale said. "Do you have a moment to talk? I just have a few questions for you."

"Sure," Oliver said, trying to hide his surprise. What could this be about? Oliver had been with another firm several years ago when a group of SEC investigators had come calling. That visit had ended with two senior bankers being led away in handcuffs and the eventual collapse of that firm. But Oliver hadn't done anything wrong, or even questionable, in his entire career. Not that he knew of, at least. His work may have been boring, but it was entirely honest. He looked at Donna questioningly. "Is there a conference room free?"

"Sausalito," she said. All the firm's conference rooms were named after cities in California. Sausalito was the smallest, tucked away in a corner. It was the least showy and hence wasn't used all that often.

"Is it private?" Mr. Teasdale asked. Oliver glanced at him, his brow wrinkling in confusion. "That is, it would be best right now if nobody saw us talking," continued Mr. Teasdale. "It might raise suspicions. Ah, questions, that is."

"We can close the door," Oliver said. "There aren't any windows. Donna, I guess, hold my calls?" Oliver had never told anyone to hold his calls in his life. Did people still say that?

"Of course, Mr. Jones." She watched the men as they started down the hall. Oliver knew that the moment they were out of earshot she'd be on the phone to one of the senior partners. Or quite possibly *all* of the senior partners. Mr. Teasdale's questions weren't the only ones he was going to be answering today

The conference room was only a short walk away. Nobody gave Oliver or his visitor a second look as they went down the hallway. It wasn't unusual for Oliver to meet representatives of the firms he was researching in his office for personal interviews. "Do you work out of the San Francisco office?" Oliver asked Mr. Teasdale, although he wasn't sure whether the SEC had a field office in the city.

"I work all over," Mr. Teasdale replied.

"Will you be here long?"

"Oh, I don't think this will take very long at all."

Oliver felt the knot in his stomach start to melt away. That was exactly what he had hoped to hear. Serious SEC investigations tended to be exhaustive. There was no such thing as a short meeting if criminal activity was suspected. This was probably about some paperwork mix-up. An unsigned form or a box checked where it shouldn't have been. He might still have his job at the end of the day.

Still, the other man made him uneasy. There was something just...*off*...about him. They reached the conference room and Oliver stole another glance at the man's face as he held open the door. There was the problem, he thought. The man's skin didn't seem to fit quite right. It was almost as if he was wearing some Hollywood-type mask to make himself look like someone else. A disguise. Oliver recalled that there had been a string of bank robberies in Southern California recently with that as the *modus operandi*. Some crafty thief had been disguising himself as an old man to fool the police into looking for someone that looked nothing like him. It was a clever idea, Oliver thought. Had they ever caught that guy?

Oliver shut the conference room door behind them. They were alone now. Mr. Teasdale looked around appraisingly. It was a simple room. There was a single rectangular wooden table surrounded by six leather chairs. A speakerphone console sat in the center of the table, and a rarely-used videoconferencing system had been pushed into the corner of the room. Oliver couldn't remember the last time anyone had needed to use it. It had been purchased in the heady *dot com* days when everyone had been flush with cash, and had been gathering dust ever since.

"Very good," Mr. Teasdale said, looking carefully at the ceiling. "I notice no security cameras in the room. None on the walls, and none in the ceiling. Is that also your understanding, Mr. Jones?"

Oliver frowned. "No, not in the conference rooms." He thought about it. "Ah...there are some out front, in reception, and in the hallways. And on the trading floor, of course, but not in here." Was that a problem? Could that be why Teasdale was here? "Do we need them?" Oliver asked. "I know the firm takes SEC regulations very seriously, so if we're violating some rule, I'm sure we'll fix it right away."

"Oh, that's quite all right." Mr. Teasdale sat his briefcase down on the table and opened it. "I suppose you're wondering what all this is about?" he asked.

"Of course," Oliver said.

Mr. Teasdale removed a small device the size and shape of a smartphone from his briefcase. He thumbed a switch on its side and Oliver could hear it begin to hum quietly.

"What is that?" Oliver asked. "Did you want to record our conversation? I should probably ask Legal to join us, then."

"I'm not going to record anything," Mr. Teasdale said. "The whole point is not to. Hence the question about the cameras."

"Then what is that thing?" Oliver gestured at the device, which was humming louder now. *Wait a minute*, he thought. What had Teasdale just said about not recording anything?

"You know what a Taser is, I assume?" Mr. Teasdale asked.

"Of course I know what a Taser is."

"It's a bit like that," Mr. Teasdale allowed. Then he pressed the end of the device firmly against Oliver's chest and pressed the trigger.

Chapter 3

Oliver was thrown backward as if he had just been kicked by a horse. His skin burned. He felt like his entire body had been dunked in gasoline and then set ablaze all at once. Then, as quickly as it had come, the pain was gone. Oliver found himself lying on the floor, numb. He was unable to move; his arms and legs felt like they had the consistency of jelly.

Mr. Teasdale was standing over him. He looked down at Oliver with a gentle expression. "I am sorry about that, Mr. Jones, but I do need you to be still for the next part."

"Guh," Oliver said. His lips refused to form words and his tongue felt like it was the size of a sweat sock.

"Yes, I suppose so," nodded Mr. Teasdale. He went to the table and placed the Taser device, or whatever it was, back in his briefcase, then removed a small syringe.

What on earth was going on? Oliver wanted to scream, to call out for security, or the police, or anyone at all, but the wind had been knocked out of him and he could barely make a sound.

Mr. Teasdale returned to where Oliver lay and knelt down carefully next to his legs. He gently slipped off Oliver's left shoe, followed by the sock. He glanced up at Oliver's questioning face. "Heart attack," he said, holding up the syringe so Oliver could see it. "Don't worry, Mr. Jones. It won't hurt much." Mr. Teasdale frowned thoughtfully. "Well, that's not exactly true. But it will be over very quickly." He spread Oliver's first and second toes apart and aimed the syringe carefully at the web of skin between them.

"I?" Oliver asked.

"Hmm?"

Oliver felt his skin beginning to tingle. Sensation was returning to his arms and legs, albeit slowly. He couldn't move his fingers, but he was able to force his mouth to form one word: "Why?"

"Oh," Mr. Teasdale nodded. "Why." He shrugged. "I honestly have no idea. It's just a job, Mr. Jones."

Oliver desperately tried to kick his left leg away from the other man, but it was his right leg that moved. Mr. Teasdale looked at him in surprise. "Impressive," he said. "I've never seen anyone recover from my stunner that quickly. It won't be quickly enough, of course." He moved the needle to within a hair's breadth of the space between Oliver's toes.

He was about to die, Oliver thought. What a stupid thing to have happen. But an instant before Mr. Teasdale could give him the injection, the conference room door flew open. Oliver tried to turn his head. Someone must have heard him fall, he thought. He was saved! But it was the man in the Hawaiian shirt that was standing there in the doorway. He held a small pistol aimed at Mr. Teasdale's head. "Drop it," he said.

Mr. Teasdale regarded the newcomer with interest. "Curiouser and curiouser," he said. "What are *you* doing here?"

"Put the syringe down," the man in the Hawaiian shirt said.

"I will not."

"Last warning."

"You know that's not going to kill me," Mr. Teasdale said. "Leave now and I'll…"

"Help me!" cried Oliver, finally finding his voice.

The man in the Hawaiian shirt gritted his teeth, and then pulled the trigger. The pistol made a noise no louder than a quiet sneeze and Mr. Teasdale was struck in the head. The impact sounded like a watermelon being hit with a baseball bat. Teasdale crumpled to the ground next to Oliver.

It was over. "Help me," Oliver repeated, relieved.

The man in the Hawaiian shirt tucked his pistol into a belt holster that had been concealed under his shirt, then moved to Oliver's side. "Can you stand?" he asked.

Oliver wasn't sure. The tingling in his extremities had faded, and it seemed like his body was starting to respond to him. With the other man's help he managed to roll over and climb to his feet, but his balance was off and his legs were shaky. It was a little like being drunk, he thought. He hadn't been drunk in years, but he was pretty sure this was what it had been like.

The man in the Hawaiian shirt held Oliver by the arm. "Good job," he said. "He hit you pretty good, looks like. It'll wear off in another couple of minutes."

"Who are you?" Oliver asked.

"I'm Tyler," the man in the Hawaiian shirt said. "Nice to meet you. Well, nice to meet you again. Now come on. We have to get out of here."

As much as Oliver wanted to be somewhere far away from here, he knew he couldn't leave the scene of his own attempted murder. "I can't go," he said. "I have to call the police."

Tyler shook his head. "Look, I hate to rush you before you're ready, but we don't have a lot of time here. He's not going to be down long."

Oliver stared at him in disbelief. The would-be killer had just been shot in the head! But then out of the corner of his eye he saw the other man stir. Oliver took an unsteady step closer and looked down at him. Had the movement been a reflex act? He had read somewhere that bodies could keep moving on their own for a few minutes after death. It was weird and unsettling to see, but entirely natural.

But then the assassin drew a sudden breath and moaned. Oliver jerked backwards in surprise. He was sure the man had not been breathing a moment ago. He could clearly see where the impact from the bullet had punched a hole in the man's skull, but something about it wasn't right. Oliver leaned closer. The wound was changing shape. "My god," Oliver said. There was no doubt about it. The wound was getting smaller, the damaged skin and bone slowly knitting back together.

Mr. Teasdale was healing from a bullet wound to the skull.

Oliver gaped. "Come on," Tyler said, pulling Oliver toward the door.

"But…"

"Questions later." Tyler pushed Oliver out of the conference room, where he promptly fell to the ground, his legs numb and twitching again. "God damn it," said Tyler. "Come on, buddy." He pulled the shaky Oliver to his feet.

The two men lumbered down the hallway together as awkwardly as children in a three-legged race. Behind them Oliver could hear Teasdale moan again, but this time he sounded stronger. Or maybe angrier? He sounded like someone who had just woken up with the world's worst hangover. Maybe that was what being shot in the head felt like.

They reached the lobby and Oliver promptly fell down again. He saw Donna was now standing behind her desk, her phone's handset pressed tightly to her ear. No doubt calling the police, Oliver thought. Thank goodness.

Two of the firm's senior partners were also in the lobby. "What's going on here?" one of them demanded. It was Mr. Peters, Oliver realized, a man who rarely left his office unless it was to fire someone. That was a task he had always seemed to enjoy.

"I don't know," Oliver said truthfully. He tried to get to his feet, but suddenly found he'd forgotten how to stand. What *was* that thing Mr. Teasdale had used on him?

Tyler pressed the elevator call button. "There's a man back there with a gun!" he said to Donna, pointing back down the hall. "I think he's crazy or something!"

"He's wearing a Hawaiian shirt," Donna said into the phone. "He has a hostage, and he says he has a gun."

"Oh, come on," Tyler complained. "I'm the good guy

here!"

The elevator chimed as its doors slid open. Tyler took Oliver by the wrist and dragged him into the elevator, hitting the button for the parking garage with his elbow.

"Stop right there!" Mr. Peters commanded, stepping forward threateningly.

Tyler took the pistol from his waistband and showed it to everyone. Nobody moved as the elevator doors slid shut.

Tyler helped Oliver to his feet once more. "You doing all right, buddy?"

Oliver's legs felt more solid under him now. He pushed Tyler away. "Who the hell are you?"

"Tyler Jacobsen. Nice to meet you, Ollie."

Nobody ever called Oliver "Ollie," but pointing that out to Tyler didn't seem all that important right now. "Okay, Tyler. Who was that up there? What's happening?"

Tyler sighed. "Look, it's a really long story. Short version: Mr. Teasdale was sent to kill you. I was sent to keep you alive. I had planned to watch you for a while but when I saw he was making a move I had to step in." He mulled that over for a moment. "Huh. You know, that was most of it, actually. I guess it wasn't that long a story after all."

"I'm calling the police," Oliver said. He reached in his front pocket but his cell phone was gone. Had someone taken it? No, it was back in his office. He'd forgotten to take it along when he left for lunch. Well, he wasn't going back upstairs to get it now. Not until Mr. Teasdale was long gone.

"Call the police and you'll be dead in an hour," Tyler said.

"Mr. Teasdale can walk into a police station as easily as he walked into your office."

Oliver shook his head. "This has to be a mistake. Assassins don't just walk into the financial district and kill people."

"One just tried to," Tyler pointed out.

"And why would anyone want to kill me?" Oliver asked. "I'm...well, I'm *me*."

"That I don't know. My orders are to take you back to my boss. She wants to talk to you. We'll keep you safe, I promise."

Oliver doubted he wanted to meet this man's boss, but they were nearly to the garage now. Oliver resolved to make a break for it once the doors opened. If his legs held up he could probably get away, or at least cause enough commotion to scare this lunatic away from him. But when the elevator stopped and the doors slid open a woman was waiting for them. She had shoulder-length red hair the color of a sunset and sharp, angular features. Oliver thought she would have been quite pretty if she smiled, but at the moment she was scowling fiercely. And scowling at *him*, Oliver noted. What had he done to deserve *that*?

The woman glared at Tyler, her emerald green eyes accusing. "Why is he still conscious?" she asked, jerking her head in Oliver's direction.

"It's fine," Tyler said. "There's no need to..."

"I don't have time for this," the woman cut him off. She took a small canister of what looked like breath spray from inside her black leather jacket and pointed it at Oliver. "Ssh," she said, pressing the trigger.

A wet cloud of mist engulfed Oliver's face. It smelled like

flowers, he thought. *Lilacs.* Was it her perfume? Then his legs felt weak again and he was falling, the world around him fading into blackness.

Chapter 4

Oliver woke up in a hospital bed, his mouth dry and the faint smell of lilacs still lingering in the back of his nose. He was surrounded by medical equipment, but the room was strangely quiet. Sitting up, he realized that he was not actually connected to any of the monitoring equipment, nor were any of the machines even turned on.

This wasn't even a real hospital room, for that matter. The bed itself and the machines looked authentic enough, but they were set up inside an ordinary bedroom. A few chairs and a small square table had been arranged next to the bed, but this room was definitely in someone's house, not in a hospital.

There was a small window next to the bed. In the distance Oliver could see the Golden Gate Bridge, barely visible through the fog. From the angle of the view he guessed that he must be somewhere in Russian Hill. Tyler and that angry woman with him must have brought him here while he was unconscious. What had been in the little canister the woman had carried? Gas? Anesthetic?

It was still daylight outside. He couldn't have been knocked out for more than a few hours. Would that have been enough time for the police to start looking for him? They might still be taking witness statements back at his office.

Oliver got out of the bed and stood up carefully. His legs were steady under him, but he found that he felt a little groggy. Whether that was from sleeping or a side effect of whatever he'd been sprayed with, he didn't know.

He wondered what he should do next. Look for the front door? Look for the *back* door? What were the odds that he was alone in this house?

That question was quickly answered for him when the bedroom door swung open and Tyler entered. He was carrying two cans of diet soda and looked genuinely pleased to see Oliver. "Oh good, you're up."

"I am," Oliver admitted.

Tyler handed Oliver one of the soda cans. Oliver noted that it had not been opened, but he had no intention of drinking it anyway. Who knew what they might have done to it?

"How are you feeling?" Tyler asked.

"I'm all right," Oliver replied, placing the can on the bedside table. "What did you do to me? Where am I?"

"You've had a rough day." Tyler looked sympathetic.

Oliver shook his head. He'd been hoping for something a little more straightforward. "Okay, look, I'm not sure who all of you think I am, but I'm not. If you're thinking of holding me for ransom you've got the wrong idea here. I don't have money. This is a mistake."

"It's complicated," Tyler allowed. "This *could* all be a mistake, actually, but Mr. Teasdale was about ten seconds away from killing you this morning, and he will definitely try again. There's no mistake about *that*."

Another encounter with the assassin was the last thing Oliver wanted, but he definitely needed to get away from this place before someone else reached for a spray can and knocked him out again. "Thanks for your help, then, but I think it's time for me to go."

"No," Tyler shook his head. "Bad idea. You're safe here."

"I'm safe?" Oliver nearly laughed. "You drugged me!"

Tyler sighed. "Yeah, I'm sorry about that. Sally can be a little...impatient. She's very good at what she does, though."

"And what does she do?"

"Well, mostly she shoots things," Tyler admitted.

Oliver didn't find that particularly reassuring. He decided to try a different tack. "Where are we?" he asked, motioning at the view out the window.

"Someplace safe, like I said. Artemis will explain everything."

"Who?"

"Is he up yet?" a female voice called. Oliver winced. He recognized that voice. He'd been hoping she was somewhere far away, but the woman who had gassed him earlier entered the room a moment later, still wearing the leather jacket she'd had on the first time he'd seen her. She looked him over appraisingly. "Good. Let's go. Artemis is waiting for you."

"I'm not going anywhere with you," Oliver told them both.

"You kidnapped me! And *you* drugged me!" he said to Sally.

"Is that all?" asked the woman, barely suppressing a laugh.

Oliver took a step toward Tyler. He seemed the more reasonable of the two of them. "Look," he said calmly, "just let me go now and I won't tell the police about you. Not your names, not about this house. I promise." Oliver hoped the man couldn't tell that he was lying. He fully intended to call the police, the FBI, and anyone else he could think of. He'd start making calls as soon as he could find a pay phone.

"You're coming downstairs now," Sally said. "This can be easy or it can be hard." She shrugged and cracked her knuckles. "I like hard, myself, but I'll let you pick."

"That's not necessary," Tyler told her. "Let's all take a breath and..."

"Sally?" a new voice called from farther away. "*Now.*"

Oliver was startled. That new voice had belonged to a child. A girl, or a small boy whose voice hadn't started to change. What the hell was going on here? Who did these people take orders from?

Tyler looked distinctly uncomfortable. "Artemis doesn't like to be kept waiting," he said.

Sally took a silver pistol out of her jacket pocket and held it up for Oliver to see. "Last chance," she said.

"You're not going to shoot me," Oliver said.

Sally's expression changed to one of amusement. "I'm not?"

"Don't be stupid," Oliver replied. He saw Tyler's mouth drop open in surprise. Oliver wasn't sure where his newfound confidence was coming from, but he'd been backed into a corner and he wasn't willing to be a victim anymore. "You people may be nuts, but you didn't go to all this trouble so you could shoot me now." It was a logical conclusion, but while Oliver was secretly pleased with his own bravado, he did wonder if provoking a crazy woman with a gun was especially wise.

"He's got you there," Tyler agreed. He had a small smile on his face. "You can't shoot him."

"I could shoot him in the arm," Sally pointed out, as if where to shoot someone was the kind of decision she had to make regularly.

"And he could bleed out," Tyler said. "Besides, if you get blood on the floor of this house, Artemis is going to have you up here with a mop and a bucket."

"Screw that," Sally said. "Fine." She put the gun away and stepped up to Oliver, close enough that he could smell that she'd been chewing breath mints recently. "You coming?"

"No."

Sally punched him hard in the gut, her fist moving so fast Oliver hadn't even seen the blow coming. He fell to his knees in pain, the wind knocked out of him for the second time that day. "Jesus," he wheezed. The woman was *strong*.

"Bang!" Sally said, throwing her arms in the air as if she'd just scored a touchdown.

"Damn it, Sally," Tyler protested. "You didn't have to do that."

"No, but I *wanted* to," Sally told him. "You see the difference?" She looked down at Oliver, clearly amused with herself. "You had enough?"

Oliver had never been punched in his life. Even as a child he hadn't been in so much as a playground scuffle. Now he had been hurt, but more than that, he was angry. Oliver wasn't sure that he had ever felt rage before, but now his chest felt like it was on fire. These people had abducted him, and now they thought they could beat him? He had no intention of trying to fight with them, but if he was going to escape, he was clearly going to have to go through them to do it. Once upon a time that thought might have bothered him. He found it didn't anymore.

He looked up at the sneering woman. "I don't think so," he said.

Sally cocked her head at him. "You've got some balls," she said. "I can respect..." but she was cut off as Oliver suddenly launched his body at her midsection. "Hey!" she yelled as he wrapped his arms around her, forcing her backwards. "Get off me!"

Oliver had only intended to knock Sally off balance so he could get past her and to the door, but his momentum had carried him too far and they fell to the floor together in a tangle of arms and legs. Sally managed to free one of her arms and fired an elbow into the side of Oliver's head. His vision filled with stars.

"Hey! Hey!" Tyler shouted. He put his arms around Oliver's torso and tried to separate the two of them. "Stop it! Break it up!" He pulled Oliver backwards away from the furious woman.

Sally scrambled to her knees and aimed a punch at Oliver's crotch. She missed, catching him instead on the inside of his thigh. Oliver felt a dull pain at the impact and his leg went numb.

Tyler managed to get between them and held them apart at arm's length. "Stop it now!" he said. "This is over!"

Oliver wanted nothing more than for it to be over, but Sally had retrieved her pistol and leveled it at Oliver's head. "Ssh," she said, her eyes fiery. He knew she was going to shoot him this time.

"Enough," a new voice commanded. The three of them looked to the door. A girl of about ten years old stood there. She had long blond hair reaching down to her waist with bangs that nearly covered her icy blue eyes. Oliver noted with some surprise that she was wearing a brown Girl Scout uniform, which seemed bizarrely out of place given the setting.

Sally didn't lower her gun. "He hit me," she told the girl. "This bastard *hit* me."

"You hit him first," the little girl observed.

"But…"

"Put the gun down now, Sally." The child's face was expressionless, but her eyes were hard. There was something profoundly disturbing about her, Oliver thought. She was like one of those creepy kids in a horror movie that turns out to be the real monster at the end.

Sally lowered the weapon. Oliver stared at her in surprise. So the child was their boss? Who the hell were these people? Some kind of cult? Did they think the kid was their messiah? Oh, that would just be perfect. God only knew what they wanted him for. Some bizarre ritual, maybe?

"Good," the little girl said primly. "Sally, go outside and

take a walk. Don't come back until you've calmed down."

Sally glared at her, then at Oliver, and then turned on her heel and left the room. Oliver could hear her footsteps going down a flight of wooden stairs. A moment later a door opened and then slammed shut.

The little girl glanced at Tyler. "I believe I said something about keeping her under control?"

"I'm sorry," Tyler said glumly. "I've been trying, but it's…"

"No, it's my fault," she interrupted. "I should have sent her to the island, but I thought keeping busy might help her work through her grief." She shook her head. "Clearly I was wrong."

"She needs time," Tyler said. "That's all."

"Time is a luxury we rarely have in this business," the girl noted.

Oliver was eyeing the door speculatively when the girl turned to him. "Mr. Jones, I apologize for my employee's indiscretion. Please come downstairs now. You will not be harmed again. At least, not by anyone here. I give you my word on that."

Oliver wasn't sure what the word of a ten-year-old was worth, but it was better than nothing. And he'd have had to admit he was a little curious about these people now. At least he'd have more information to give to the police later. "Who are you?"

"My name is Artemis," the girl said. "And please believe me when I say that without our help, you will be dead by this time tomorrow. Will you please come downstairs and listen to me?"

Oliver decided he didn't have anything to lose by agreeing,

and getting downstairs would put him one step closer to the front door. "I'll come," he said.

"Thank you," Artemis said. "Tyler made a batch of muffins earlier. Perhaps you will have one."

Oliver blinked. "A muffin?"

"Indeed. Blueberry."

"They're good," Tyler said. "My mother's recipe."

They were definitely a cult, Oliver thought.

Chapter 5

Artemis led Oliver downstairs and showed him to a chair in the house's living room. The rest of the house seemed to be sparsely furnished with only the most basic necessities. Oliver didn't see a single photograph or family memento. There were no children's toys on the floor or paintings of long-gone relatives hanging over the mantle. There didn't seem to be a single thing in the house that could be used to identify the people that lived there.

Oliver wondered if anyone actually lived here at all. It looked more like a model home that would be shown to prospective homebuyers, except that much of the furniture seemed to belong to another time period. Like the elegant Edwardian chairs he and Artemis were sitting in now. Oliver had seen chairs like this before, but that had been on a PBS antiques show. They certainly hadn't come from one of the local furniture stores. Given their pristine condition, they must have cost a small fortune.

Tyler went into the kitchen and returned a minute later with half a dozen blueberry muffins arranged on a silver tray. He sat them on a nearby table along with a stack of small plates for serving and a dish of butter. He'd also brewed a pot of tea. Oliver didn't intend to touch any of it. The strange little girl that had been giving the orders had promised that he would be safe, but he didn't see the need to take any chances.

Oliver had taken note of the front door's location as soon as they'd reached the living room. He couldn't see whether the deadbolt was engaged, but he was encouraged to see the path to the door was both unguarded and unobstructed. He expected that he could get past the child easily enough, and Tyler had never seemed inclined to hurt him. Sally would be another matter, and she still had that gun in her jacket. If he was going to make a move, he would need to do it before she came back.

Artemis munched thoughtfully on a muffin, holding a small plate delicately beneath it to catch any crumbs that might fall. A steaming cup of tea sat on a small table next to her. She hadn't said a word to Oliver since they had come downstairs. She'd just stared at him, the way one might look at a curious work of art in a museum, or maybe a goat with two heads. Finally she sighed and put her muffin down. "Well, Mr. Jones, I give up."

"I'm sorry?" he asked. "You give up?" What was she talking about now?

"I've been thinking about this for some small while now and I can't come up with anything, so I will simply ask you outright. What exactly are you?"

Oliver frowned. There was a question nobody had ever asked him before. "Pardon me?"

"What are you?" she repeated.

Oliver thought about it. "I'm a stock analyst?" he offered, unsure as to what she wanted.

"No," she sighed, as if she were trying to explain algebra to a puppy. "That is what you *do*. The question is what you *are*. You do see the difference, I hope?"

"I'm a man?"

She thought about it. "I'm not entirely sure that is true."

Oliver suppressed a tired chuckle. That cinched it. There was no point in trying to reason with these people. They were nuts. How long would it take him to get to the door? Ten seconds? He should wait until Tyler went back into the kitchen to be on the safe side. Maybe if he asked for a soda he could get the man out of the room.

"Something very odd is going on here," Artemis continued. "You have managed to make a very powerful enemy, but I have no idea how. I was hoping you could enlighten me."

"I have no idea what is going on," Oliver said. "This day has been one crazy thing after another. First I kept running into him," he nodded at Tyler, who was standing quietly just behind Artemis with his hands clasped together in front of him.

"Tyler."

"Yes. I saw him twice this morning, first on the train and then at lunch."

"I sent him to keep an eye on you."

"Okay, fine. Then the other guy shows up at my office…"

"Mr. Teasdale."

"Yeah. He hit me with a Taser or something, and was going to inject me with…poison…I guess." Oliver paused, suddenly curious about something. "Is his name really Hilary Teasdale?"

Tyler smirked but Artemis's face remained impassive. "It is what he calls himself. It is certainly not his real name, but to be honest I'm not sure he ever had a name in the first place."

"Oh."

"Do you have any idea why he was after you?"

"No. He told me he was with the SEC, but that obviously wasn't true."

"It was not. Had you ever seen him before?"

"I don't think so."

"Take a moment to think about it. Perhaps you saw him at the grocery? Or outside your house?"

Oliver thought it over, but he was sure he'd remember someone like Mr. Teasdale. He'd found the man unsettling even before the assassin had tried to kill him, and then somehow recovered from a bullet wound in the head. "No, I'm sure I never saw him before."

"Hmm," Artemis mused. "That is odd."

Oliver glanced at the door. It had only been a longshot that one of them might have some insight, but this didn't seem to be going anywhere. He had no idea how long Sally's "walk" would last, and as much as he had questions he wanted answers to, he'd probably wasted enough time here. "So, thank you," he said, "but I'm going to go now." Oliver stood up, watching Tyler carefully for any reaction. The other man didn't move. "I don't want to hurt either of you, so please don't try to stop me."

"Very well," Artemis said. "Goodbye, Mr. Jones."

Oliver stared at her. That was it? "You're letting me go?"

"Yes." She took a sip of her tea. "Oh, that is quite good," she said. "Thank you, Tyler," she nodded at him. Oliver saw the other man beaming.

"You're serious? I can go? Just like that?" This had to be some kind of trick, Oliver thought.

"Just like that."

Oliver looked at Tyler again, but the man only nodded toward the door. "Tyler will not stand in your way," Artemis assured him.

Oliver took a step toward the door, then stopped. Nobody moved. He took another, but neither of them seemed to care if he left. If this had been a kidnapping, it was the worst one in history. They hadn't made any ransom demands. Instead they'd offered him muffins and tea. And now they were letting him go.

Nobody at work was ever going to believe this. The police would never believe this. How on earth was he going to keep from getting fired?

"Well, goodbye," Oliver said when he reached the door. He tried the doorknob and was surprised to find it unlocked.

"Goodbye," Artemis said.

Still wondering if someone new was about to appear and tackle him to the ground, Oliver hesitantly stepped through the door.

Chapter 6

Oliver closed the door gently behind him. He listened at the door for a moment, but could hear no sounds coming from inside. There were no raised voices. No commotion as someone raced for the door. Nobody seemed to be coming after him at all.

He stepped away from the door and headed down the stone walkway toward the street. At first he didn't notice anything amiss. This was definitely Russian Hill, he thought; he recognized the neighborhood. There was a little hole-in-the-wall Vietnamese restaurant he liked not far from here. Not far from *there* was Van Ness, a major thoroughfare that ran through San Francisco. It would be easy enough to hail a cab once he got there. He could be at a police station fifteen minutes from now. He'd be safe there while this mess got sorted out.

It was then that he noticed the cars. There were several of them in the street, just as he would have expected there to be on any day of the week, but at the moment none of them were moving. That was definitely odd for this time of day. He looked to the left and the right, but couldn't see a reason why the cars would have stopped. There were no obstacles in the street, no detours or construction that he could see, and there weren't nearly enough cars for there to be any kind of congestion.

Oliver hesitated for a moment, then carefully stepped into the street. He approached the nearest car and bent down to peek inside. He could see the driver inside talking on his cell phone, his mouth open wide in laughter. But the man's mouth wasn't moving. No part of him was moving, for that matter. The man was frozen in place.

A short distance up the street Oliver could see another man on the sidewalk. He must have been walking, but had stopped in midstride, one foot stuck barely an inch above the ground. Just behind him Oliver could see a letter carrier stooping down to open a mailbox, his key inserted halfway into the lock but not going any further. Everyone he could see was as still as a mannequin, frozen in a bizarre approximation of everyday life.

It wasn't just the people, Oliver realized. *Nothing* was moving. A man to his left had been out walking his dog, but the dog was just as still now as the man. Just in front of him Oliver could see a leaf which had been in the process of falling from a tree. It had stopped in mid-air. Oliver took a step forward, so close that he could have kissed it if he'd wanted to, then he cautiously reached up and tried to pluck it out of the air. He felt it resist for a moment, as if the leaf were stuck in molasses, and then it came free. He stared at it in his hand. It was just an ordinary leaf. What was going on here?

"What on earth?" he asked aloud. His voice sounded oddly resonant. He quickly realized it was because nothing else in the neighborhood was making a sound. The entire world around him was deathly silent.

"It's like walking into a painting," Tyler said from behind him. Oliver nearly jumped in surprise. The other man was standing a few feet away, looking up at a bird frozen in mid-flight above them. "It's wild, isn't it?"

"What is this?" Oliver asked in wonderment.

"Oh, I can't tell you exactly," Tyler admitted. "I asked Artemis once and she tried to explain it to me, but theoretical physics is way outside my area."

"But you're doing this? Controlling it?"

"Oh, no. That's way beyond our abilities, believe me. You see that house?" he pointed at the building they had just left. "It exists at a single fixed point in time. From its perspective the outside world never moves and never changes. So we use it as a safe house. It's a great place to hide for a while."

"A fixed point in time?" Oliver asked. "So…is this the past? Or the future?" Oliver was beginning to think he'd need a physics textbook to understand all of this. Or possibly some LSD.

"No, we're still in the same time we left. Inside the house it's the past. Or the future. I'm not actually sure *when* the house is. But out here, everything is back to normal."

"This isn't normal," Oliver said, looking around. "Nothing is moving." A frightening thought occurred to him. "Wait, are we stuck like this?"

"No. Now that you're outside you'll catch up to the rest of the universe. Or it will catch up to you. I don't know. It just takes a minute, though. There, see?" He pointed to the street.

Oliver looked. The cars he had been so fascinated by earlier were beginning to move. They were moving very slowly, but it was still movement none the same. As he watched, they slowly began to speed up. It was like seeing a movie that had been playing in slow-motion, but was slowly winding up to the correct speed.

"Unbelievable," Oliver said.

"Yeah. This kind of thing, you get used to it," Tyler shrugged. "Look, I'm not going to force you, but would you please come back in and listen to what Artemis has to say? I know none of us has much of a bedside manner, but we're actually trying to help you out here."

Oliver thought about it. One of two things was certain. Either he was losing his mind, or something truly strange was really happening, something that went well beyond anything he could understand without help. These people were very, very odd, and for all he knew they really were part of a cult, but they couldn't make time stop. And they were the only people here offering to help him.

"I'll come inside," Oliver said. He looked past Tyler, only to see the house he had just come from was gone. Only an empty lot stood there now.

"It's still there," Tyler said, anticipating Oliver's next question. "It's back to normal out here, so you can't see it anymore." Indeed, Oliver could see that things outside had returned to the way they had been before. The cars in the street were once again moving at normal speeds, and the dog walker had just passed by them with no indication that he had ever seen anything amiss.

"Why not?" Oliver asked.

"Because it doesn't exist in this timeline," Tyler explained. "It hasn't been built yet. Or it has already been torn down. Or maybe it was never built here at all." He frowned and scratched his head. "God, I hate this time stuff. Sometimes I expect to come out of there and run straight into a pack of dinosaurs."

Oliver wondered if that were possible. "How do we get back inside, then?"

"The way this works," Tyler started to explain, "no, that's not it. Let me think. Okay. See, *you* exist in *its* timeline now. Even though it doesn't exist for the rest of the world, you'll be able to see it if you can remember that it's there. Think about it for a minute. Do you remember the house being there?"

"Yes."

"What kind of house was it?"

Oliver thought it over. "I don't know anything about architecture," he said finally. "It was grey. It had two stories."

"Okay, that should be enough. Can you remember what it looked like, in your mind?"

"Yeah."

"Look for it now."

Oliver looked at the empty lot again, fully expecting to see nothing. But now the odd grey house stood there again. Oliver felt a chill. He had a feeling that somehow the house had been there since the beginning of time, and would remain there until time's end.

"There you go," said Tyler. "Let's go inside."

Oliver hesitated, but he'd come this far. What did he have to lose now? He followed Tyler up the walkway and into the house.

Artemis was still seated in the living room, not having moved from her chair. She was sipping her tea thoughtfully. "I trust now we can talk without you bolting for the door?"

"We can talk," Oliver said.

"Excellent. Do have one of Tyler's muffins. They're quite good, and by now you must know that if we wanted to harm you, we wouldn't need to resort to poison."

She had a point, Oliver thought. He took a muffin from the table and poured himself a cup of tea, then returned to his chair and sat down facing the little girl. A tentative bite was enough for him to tell that the muffin he'd taken was both moist and delicious. "Oh!" he said. "These really are good."

Tyler beamed. "I told you," Artemis said.

Chapter 7

"So," Oliver began. "Who exactly are you people?" A thought suddenly occurred to him, one that would have seemed ludicrous as recently as fifteen minutes ago, but given the circumstances now seemed at least somewhat plausible. "Of course. You're time travelers. From the future?"

Tyler laughed out loud and Oliver thought he saw a hint of a smile on the little girl's face. "No, Mr. Jones, we are not. Are you, by any chance?"

"No." Oliver was a bit disappointed. It had been an interesting idea. When he'd been younger he'd been fascinated by time travel stories and old *Doctor Who* episodes.

"I see," Artemis said. "It might have helped to answer some questions if you were, but I was fairly certain you were not. I might return to my earlier question…"

"What am I?"

"Yes," she continued. "But I suspect that you yourself do not know the answer."

"Why do you keep asking me that?" Oliver asked.

"Because you made it onto Mr. Teasdale's target list," the girl explained. "That virtually guarantees that there's something special about you."

"Because an assassin came after me?"

"That would be mundane. Assassins kill people all the time, as I understand it. But Mr. Teasdale is something of a specialist, you see. Only the more exotic targets are of any interest to him. He wouldn't accept a contract for anything less."

"Oh."

"So what is it that makes you exotic, Mr. Jones?"

"Nothing." Oliver shrugged, genuinely stumped. "I'm not exotic. I'm just some guy. I'm boring."

"At least part of that is true," Artemis nodded. "You are, in fact, extremely boring. Tyler?"

Tyler went into the kitchen and emerged with a thin manila folder. He handed it to Artemis, who opened it on her lap and looked through the contents.

"What is that?" Oliver asked.

"Your file."

"You people have a file on me?"

"We did do our research, of course," Artemis said. "Although I must admit your file is unusually thin." She thumbed through the pages. "Dead-end job. No intimate relationships. No friends."

"I have friends," Oliver protested.

"You have people you know," Artemis noted. "You don't have friends."

Oliver opened his mouth, but then shut it again. He didn't have a good comeback for that.

"You work, eat, and sleep." She looked up at him. "Am I missing anything? You don't even appear to have a hobby."

Oliver didn't care for her tone, but he didn't have anything to say in his defense. He wished he had signed up for that cooking class he had been thinking about taking. That would have shown her.

"There *is* something strange about you," Artemis continued. "I'm sure of that." She studied his face for a moment, but then shook her head. "I can't tell what it is. You look like..." she trailed off.

"Like what?" Oliver asked.

"Like someone who does not fit into this world," Artemis said.

Oliver blinked. "What does that mean?"

"I'm not sure," she said.

"Are you psychic at all?" Tyler asked suddenly.

"Psychic? Are you saying psychics are real?" Oliver started to smirk, thinking of late-night infomercials he'd seen, but Tyler just nodded at him. "Oh. You were serious. No, I'm not psychic."

"An alien?"

"You're joking now."

"He's not," Artemis said, "although that would be a little

far-fetched."

"I'm not an alien." Oliver said, annoyed.

"He could be an alien and not know it," Tyler said to Artemis.

"I'm not a damn alien!"

"Cyborg?" asked Tyler.

"There aren't any cyborgs," Artemis told him.

"Not anymore," said Sally from the doorway. Oliver had to stifle a gasp. He hadn't heard the door opening or her coming inside.

"Not anymore," Artemis repeated quietly.

Oliver thought he heard regret in the little girl's voice. "What happened to the cyborgs?" he asked. Then he pondered how insane that question sounded.

"I killed them," Sally said simply.

"Oh," Oliver said. That wasn't exactly what he had expected to hear. Of course, a minute ago he wouldn't have expected to hear that there had *ever* been cyborgs.

"We're getting off the subject," Artemis said. "Is there anything strange in your life you can think of that defies an easy explanation? Odd coincidences? Anything that happened that seemed too good, or too bad, to be true? Prophetic dreams?"

"I don't dream," Oliver said.

"You…" Artemis blinked in surprise. "You what?"

"I don't dream," Oliver repeated. "I never have."

"You probably have dreams and just don't remember them," Tyler suggested.

"No, I've never dreamed. I'm sure of it." For as long as he'd lived, Oliver had never had a dream. He wasn't sure he was missing anything. Given the state of his life, any dreams he had were bound to be pretty dull.

Artemis mulled that over. "Interesting, but not symptomatic of anything I can think of. Except perhaps brain damage."

"I don't have brain damage," Oliver said.

"Then what is it that separates you from any other lonely, single stock analyst with no friends?"

Oliver opened his mouth to say something rude, but suddenly stopped. He had just remembered something.

Artemis saw it on his face. "What?" She leaned forward, pointing her index finger at him. "What did you think of just now?"

Oliver didn't want to say it out loud. "It's nothing. Just something I imagined."

"Say it!" the little girl warned.

Oliver sighed. This had already been the strangest conversation of his life. What did he have to lose? "A cat talked to me," he admitted.

Sally snorted in derision and Tyler looked away. Oliver could tell he was trying not to grin. "A cat talked to you," Artemis repeated.

"Yes." Oliver already wished he hadn't mentioned it.

"Cats cannot speak, Mr. Jones," the girl said dryly.

"Yeah, I guess not."

"Well," Artemis said thoughtfully, "that's not entirely true. However, the last cat that *could* speak died over two thousand years ago."

"Really?" asked Tyler, perking up instantly. "That's amazing."

"Not really," Artemis said. "The poor thing's brain was so scrambled from generations of inbreeding, she never made much sense."

Tyler and Sally stared at Artemis, who ignored them. "As I said, Mr. Jones, cats cannot speak. So perhaps that much was your imagination, after all."

"Okay," Oliver said, hoping that meant they could change the subject.

"Out of curiosity, what did the cat say?"

"Jeffrey," Oliver corrected her. Artemis raised her eyebrows curiously at him. "I named him Jeffrey," he explained. When she didn't reply, Oliver continued, hoping he wasn't about to be laughed at again. "He said that my life wouldn't be easier if he could talk."

"I see. That is an unusual way to begin a conversation. May I assume you spoke to... *Jeffrey*...first?"

"Yeah."

"And you said to him?"

Oliver sighed. "I told him I wished he could talk."

"And then he spoke."

"Yeah."

"So in a way," Artemis mused, "your wish was granted."

"He's a genie!" Tyler exclaimed, pointing at Oliver triumphantly. Artemis turned and glared at him. "Sorry," he said sheepishly.

Artemis turned back to Oliver. She made her fingers into a steeple and said nothing for a long moment. Finally she looked up. "I don't know what to make of this, honestly. But I've decided that we will continue to protect you for the time being. Mr. Teasdale's clients tend to be extremely unpleasant people, and I've found that the world is a better place when they don't get what they want. If one of them wants you dead, I want you alive. For now, at least."

Oliver thought he saw Sally brighten up at the "for now" but he decided not to make an issue of it. "So what am I supposed to do?" he asked. "Hide here?

"No," Artemis replied. "This house can only be used for short periods of time or else...*things* happen. And Mr. Teasdale is hunting you. I don't want him tracking you here."

"Can he see the house?" Sally asked.

"Not yet," Artemis replied. "But given enough time, he would be able to discern that it is here."

"So I should..." Oliver began, hoping she would finish the sentence for him.

"We will need to figure out who hired him," Artemis said. "Who is it that wants you dead?"

"Besides Sally?" Oliver asked.

Oliver thought he saw another trace of a smile from the

girl. "Yes. Besides her." She rubbed her palms together. "Well, there is work to be done. Tyler, go to it. Take him with you and try to keep him alive."

"Got it," Tyler said.

"What about me?" Sally asked.

"You will drive me back to the office," Artemis said. "We have a matter to discuss."

Sally didn't look pleased, but Oliver noted that she didn't argue with the girl. He was a bit relieved that she wasn't coming along with them. He wouldn't have to worry about getting on her bad side. But he still had questions before he took off with Tyler.

"Wait a minute here," Oliver said. "What about my...my life? My house? My job? How am I going to explain all this to people at work?"

"I don't know," Artemis said, standing up. "But I am certain that it will be much more difficult to explain if you are dead. For now, Mr. Jones, I will ask you to trust us."

"And everything will be okay, I guess?" he asked, feeling a bit of sarcasm might be called for.

"Things rarely are," Artemis said, heading for the door. Sally trailed a step behind the girl. A moment later they had both vanished through the door, back into the real world.

"Now what?" Oliver asked Tyler.

"I'm going to do the dishes," Tyler said, collecting the muffin plates and tea cups onto the tray and taking them into the kitchen.

"Oh." That seemed awfully mundane given that they were

inside a house where time stood still, but Oliver guessed that household chores were the same wherever, or *whenever* you were. "And then?"

"Then we're going to go find out who wants to kill you," Tyler called from the kitchen. "You want me to pack up some of these muffins for later?"

Oliver was about to say "no" when he caught himself. "Yes," he said. "Yes I do."

Chapter 8

As a child, Oliver had been enamored of fairy tales. One of his favorites had opened with the line, "Sometimes more happens in a single day than in a hundred years." What followed was the story of an ordinary villager who wound up fighting an ogre and saving a princess. Or something like that. Oliver could no longer remember exactly how the story had gone. Whatever it had been, Oliver had decided he was having that kind of day. When he'd gone to work this morning he'd been living an ordinary life. In the few hours since then he'd been the victim of an assassination attempt, had been gassed and sort-of kidnapped, and had eaten fantastic blueberry muffins in a house that apparently existed in its own unique corner of the space-time continuum.

Now he was on the run, and the only people he felt sure he could trust, albeit hesitantly, were a creepy little girl, a woman who had threatened to shoot him, and...Tyler. Tyler, a man who possessed a very questionable fashion sense, but made up for it with fantastic baking skills.

I'm so screwed, Oliver thought.

Tyler had driven them to the Tenderloin district in a black 1960's era Dodge Charger. Oliver had marveled at the car when he'd seen it parked outside the house. He hadn't seen one like it in years. "Did you have to go back in time to buy it?" he'd asked Tyler.

"No," Tyler had replied, looking confused. "I bought it in Oakland."

Oliver was about to say he had only been joking, but then he wondered if that was something people actually did. Go back in time to buy cars. The others had laughed at the idea of being time travelers, though, so that seemed a bit far-fetched.

At the moment Tyler was on his knees in front of the rear door of a run-down pawn shop, attempting to pick its lock. There had been a "CLOSED" sign in the front window and if there was anybody inside the store, they'd ignored Tyler's repeated banging on the front door.

"God *damn* it," Tyler swore. One of his picks had snapped.

"You've picked locks before?" Oliver asked.

"I don't make a habit of it," Tyler said, retrieving another pick from a kit he'd had stashed in his glove compartment. "He's got a good lock."

"Did it ever occur to you that he's out to lunch or something? We could just wait."

"It's not like him to close during the day," Tyler said. "Besides, you want to be hanging around here while an assassin is out looking for you? In *this* neighborhood? Somebody might beat him to killing you."

"Fair point," Oliver said. He avoided the Tenderloin as a general rule. It was as high-crime an area as could be found in San Francisco.

The lock clicked. "Finally!" Tyler announced triumphantly. He pushed the door open. "See? Nothing to it. Let's go check it out."

Oliver wasn't sure this was such a good idea. It was breaking and entering, after all. But to be fair, a minor felony was probably the least of what he had to worry about today. He stepped cautiously through the door after Tyler.

He found himself in a storage room lit by one bare, flickering bulb in the ceiling. The room was filled with metal shelves cluttered with old electronic equipment. DVD players, televisions, and old computers were stacked on top of each other in haphazard piles. In one corner he could see a man-sized gun safe. The room was covered in dust and looked as if it hadn't been cleaned in years.

Tyler had taken his pistol out from under his shirt. "Rocky?" he called. "You in here?"

The shop was quiet. Rocky, whoever he was, wasn't answering. A rectangular object caught Oliver's eye. "Is this a Betamax?" he asked quietly. "I've never seen one of these in real life."

"Might be," Tyler said. "You can ask Rocky about it."

Oliver ran his hand over the ancient video player. He was sure it was authentic. "Why would anyone hold onto this?" he wondered. "Who would buy it?"

"I don't know," Tyler said. "Probably nobody. The thing is, he's not really a pawnbroker." He looked through the doorway into the main room. "Rocky?"

"What is he really?" Oliver asked.

"He's a...aw, shit." Tyler said, spotting something. He went through the doorway.

Oliver peered through the doorway after him. Tyler was in the center of the room, kneeling down next to an overweight man in a dirty white T-shirt and jeans. The other man was balding, unshaven, and didn't appear to be breathing.

"Oh," Oliver said, feeling a knot form in his stomach.

Tyler felt the other man's neck for a pulse. "Come on, Rocky," he said quietly. He waited, but then shook his head. "Nope. He's all done."

"I'm...I'm sorry," Oliver said.

"Don't be. He was an asshole." Tyler sighed. "How was Teasdale going to do you? Injection?" He tugged at Rocky's shoe and removed it, followed by the sock. Oliver winced as Tyler pried the other man's toes apart and inspected the skin between them. "Nothing there," he said. He went to work pulling off the other shoe.

"Is that really necessary?" Oliver asked. It seemed somehow obscene to be examining a dead man's feet.

"If you want to know what's going on here, then yes. There. See?" He motioned for Oliver to look at the skin between the first two toes on Rocky's other foot. Oliver could see a tiny red mark there. "Injection site," Tyler said. "This could've been you."

Oliver felt sick. "But why?"

"Why kill you? Like I said, we don't know yet."

"No, not that. Why kill him? What does *he* have to do with this?"

Tyler stood up. "You think Mr. Teasdale is in the phone book? He's not. If you want to hire him, you need a middle man. Rocky here is...was...one."

"A middle man?"

"Yeah. A guy with connections. He knew everyone and could get you most anything. I didn't know until now he was the broker on your contract, but even if he hadn't been, it would have been a good bet he knew who was in the market for a killer."

"So why kill him?"

"The deal's gone to shit. You got away and now we're involved. If he's dead, he doesn't tell us who's behind this. I guess Mr. Teasdale didn't trust him to keep his mouth shut." He took his phone out of his pocket. "Damn it. Artemis is going to be pissed."

Tyler made a quick call, telling the little girl what had happened and listening to her instructions. He hung up with a grimace. "She's sending cleanup," he told Oliver. "You may as well look around the place, see if there's anything you want."

Oliver looked around, confused. There was nobody else working. "You mean *steal* things?"

Tyler shrugged. "Steal. Loot. It hardly matters now. Leave some money on the desk if you want." He spotted a stack of old records and started flipping through them. "You never know what he's going to have."

There was something grotesque about looking through a dead man's merchandise while the dead man in question was lying on the floor in front of them. "What did you mean by *cleanup*?" he asked.

"Grab his computers and files. I'm sure it's all encrypted but we've got a guy. There may not be much we can use, but you never know."

"Oh."

"And of course, scrub away any trace that we were ever here. Hair, fingerprints, skin cells. Anything with DNA that could lead back to us."

"You can do that?"

"Sure. It's easy, if you know how. And if you have the right tools."

Oliver didn't feel like browsing around the shop. He went to stand by the door. "How long until that team of yours gets here?"

"A few minutes." Tyler had chosen a few records and was looking through a stack of comic books. "You sure you don't want anything?"

"That man is dead!" Oliver snapped.

"And you're alive," Tyler observed. "Keep that in mind."

Oliver shook his head in disgust. He was thinking about calling his office, although he knew he didn't dare. The police must be finished over there by now. How much would they have been able to get off of the security camera footage from the lobby? If they managed to get a good photo of Mr. Teasdale, maybe they were out looking for him. Of course, that meant they were likely out looking for Tyler, too, given that Tyler was the one who had actually dragged him out of the office.

He made a mental note to update his resume when he got the chance. And he'd have to think of an answer for when somebody asked the reason he'd left his last position. He wasn't sure a story about an assassin showing up at his office was going to cut it. *Hostile work environment*, he thought. That sounded better.

"Nice!" Tyler said. He held up an old Spider-Man comic so Oliver could see it. Oliver looked at him blankly. "It's rare," Tyler said by way of explanation.

"That's great," Oliver said dryly. He didn't know of many grown men who got excited over comic books. That was stuff for kids, or people who lived in their parents' basements. But then again, maybe for people in Tyler's line of work it counted as research. The next time you had to fight a killer robot from the future, you could try doing what Superman had done in that situation. It wasn't like that kind of thing was taught in schools.

"Why do you take orders from a little girl?" Oliver asked, curious whether he could get any more information about these people.

Tyler looked up from his comic. "Let me give you some advice. Never call Artemis *little*, and never underestimate her. And for god's sake don't make her angry."

"What, she's supposed to be dangerous?"

Tyler didn't blink. "More than you can imagine."

Oliver studied the other man's face. There was no sign that he was about to grin and betray that he'd only been joking. "Okay, then."

"Okay." Tyler went back to his comic.

Minutes passed and then there was a sharp rap at the front door. "It's still locked," Tyler said. "Do you mind letting her in?"

Oliver peeked through the window. Sally was waiting there, arms folded in front of her. He wished Artemis would have sent someone else. Sally's presence here could lead to another confrontation, and he really wanted to avoid having that happen again.

Oliver unlatched the deadbolt a bit nervously and opened the door, hoping his face didn't betray the fact that he was at least a little bit afraid of her.

Sally nodded at him as she entered the shop, latching the door behind her. She didn't look happy to see him, but Oliver was pleased that the rage he'd seen in her eyes earlier was gone. He wondered if she'd ever really shot anyone with that gun she always seemed to carry, or whether that was just an act she put on to intimidate people.

No, he thought. There was no way that was an act. She had definitely shot someone. Quite possibly a lot of someones.

"His office?" she asked Tyler, completely nonplussed by the dead body in the center of the room.

"Over there," Tyler pointed. "Where's Seven?"

"Seven had a nutty. He's not coming."

"Figures," Tyler said.

"Who's Seven?" Oliver asked.

"Tech support," Tyler answered.

"I've got this covered," Sally said. "You guys can get out of here."

"We can give you a hand," Tyler offered.

"No. Artemis wants you two mobile in case you're being tracked. You have any other leads you can follow?"

Tyler shrugged. "Not really. There are some people I can talk to. Rocky was my best shot, though."

"Yeah." Sally looked at Oliver and he noticed her shoulders stiffen slightly. "I'm..." she began. "Damn it." She took a deep breath. "Oliver, I'm sorry I hit you earlier. It was uncalled for and wrong of me." The apology sounded rehearsed. Oliver wondered how long she had been working on it.

"Oh," Oliver said. "Okay. Well, I'm sorry I tackled you."

"You *tried* to tackle me," she corrected him.

"I'm sorry I *tried* to tackle you."

"Okay," she said. "Done."

Tyler stared at her in shock. "What did Artemis say to you?" he asked.

"Never mind," she said, her eyes challenging him to make an issue out of it.

Tyler looked like he wanted to say something else, but then just shrugged. "All right."

Sally nodded at Oliver again, and then went into Rocky's office. Tyler watched for a moment as she began dismantling a computer, then turned to Oliver. "Do you have any idea how long it's been since she apologized for something?" he asked quietly.

Oliver had no idea, having only met her this morning. "It's not a big deal," he said.

"It's a very big deal," Tyler disagreed. "It's progress."

"Oh?"

"Anyway, let's get going. There's nothing more for us to do here."

"Where are we going?" Oliver asked, hoping that there wouldn't be another dead body wherever they wound up.

"Trust me. I have an idea"

Chapter 9

Tyler drove them to Haight-Ashbury, a neighborhood that had been famous in the 1960's as the center of the hippie counterculture movement in San Francisco, if not the entire United States. A lot of time had passed since the "summer of love," and the neighborhood had taken a sad turn for the worse. Homeless people and drug dealers outnumbered aging hippies and curious tourists by a wide margin. The Haight was still a good place to score a little weed, if that was your thing, but it was also a good place to get robbed, or stabbed. Or possibly both at the same time.

Tyler drove up and down the streets slowly, scanning the sidewalks and trying to peer down alleyways as he did so. He was clearly looking for something. "Are you lost?" Oliver finally asked.

"No."

"What are you trying to find?"

"Not what," Tyler said. "Who. And there she is," he

pointed up the street. Oliver looked, but all he could see was a dirty teenage girl sitting on the steps outside of an apartment building. She wore ratty jeans and had a tangled mess of rainbow-colored dreadlocks running down her back. She was smoking a cigarette, taking long drags and watching the smoke thoughtfully as it rose into the sky.

"Her?" Oliver asked. "Are you kidding?"

"Nope." Tyler pulled the Charger off to the side of the road, nearly rolling one tire up onto the sidewalk.

"You're right in front of a hydrant," Oliver pointed out.

"We won't be long. You got a twenty?"

"What?"

"Twenty bucks."

"Oh. What for?"

"Never mind, just give me twenty bucks."

Oliver went into his wallet and fished out a crisp twenty-dollar bill. "Here."

"Thanks," Tyler said. "Stay here."

Tyler got out of the car and started up the sidewalk. Oliver watched as he approached the smoking girl, who stood up and smiled when she saw him. Oliver wondered how they knew each other. She couldn't just be some random homeless girl. Could she also work for Artemis? Maybe she was some kind of secret agent, working undercover.

Tyler and the girl spoke for about a minute, Tyler at one point motioning towards Oliver. Oliver saw the girl look at him. He raised his hand instinctively to wave at her, and immediately felt like an idiot for doing so. But the girl just waved back and nodded to Tyler. He handed the girl Oliver's money and started back for the car. The girl headed off in the other direction.

"Who was that?" Oliver asked as Tyler got back behind the wheel.

"Her name is Khameleon. With a *K*."

"Khameleon? Really?"

"No, of course not. I don't know her real name. That's what she's calling herself these days, so it's good enough for me."

"Oh." Oliver watched as the girl disappeared around the corner. "So does she have special powers? Her skin changes color or something?"

Tyler looked at him like he was an idiot. "No," he said slowly. "She's just a girl."

"Well it's about as plausible as a guy getting shot in the head and then getting up and walking around five minutes later," Oliver said defensively.

"Hmm. Yeah. Fair enough," Tyler admitted.

"So what was that? What is she doing now?"

"Putting the word out," Tyler said. "We need information. They have it."

"Who? Homeless drug dealers?"

"She's not a drug dealer. Well, she *is*, but not today."

"But she is homeless?" Oliver asked. He hadn't been entirely serious before.

"Yeah."

Oliver was sure he had to be missing something. "You're expecting a homeless girl to help us?"

"Exactly."

"You're serious?" *Now* who was the idiot? "You just gave her twenty bucks? You realize she's probably buying drugs right now?"

"She's not buying drugs. Come on, let's get out of here."

Tyler drove them aimlessly around San Francisco for half an hour before he finally asked, "Are you hungry? I'm hungry. Why don't we get something to eat?"

Oliver didn't feel much like eating, but the thought occurred to him that he hadn't had any food today other than Tyler's blueberry muffins. He really ought to eat something more substantial, if for no better reason than to keep his energy up. He might need to run later, particularly if he saw Mr. Teasdale again. "Sure," he said. "Why not?"

A few minutes later they were at a run-down Chinese restaurant in North Beach. At first Oliver didn't even think it was open. One of the windows had been boarded up, probably after having a rock thrown through it by vandals, and the neon "Open" sign hadn't been turned on. But there were diners inside, and a friendly Asian waitress greeted Tyler by name. He had obviously been here before. The waitress showed them to an out-of-the-way table and left to get them glasses of water.

There was a small television bolted to the wall in the corner. The local news channel had broken into whatever mindless late afternoon talk show had been on with a special alert. A small building was on fire in the Tenderloin. Oliver squinted at the television. The building looked awfully familiar to him.

"Hey, isn't that..." he trailed off, realizing what it was.

"Oh, I don't believe it," Tyler spat. "She burned it down." The news channel only had a helicopter camera shot of the blaze, but it was clearly Rocky's pawn shop, currently engulfed in a massive fire. It was clear very little would be left of the building once the firefighters had managed to put the fire out.

"Did you know she was going to do that?" Oliver asked.

"No. But it doesn't surprise me all that much."

"Do you think Artemis told her to..."

"No, but she didn't tell her *not* to either. That much is obvious." He shook his head. "This is the last thing we need."

"What?"

"Attention."

Tyler sulked until the waitress returned with their drinks, along with a serving cart holding three dishes of food. "We didn't order yet..." Oliver began, but Tyler waved him off.

"I always start with this," he said. "Thank you, Li-Jen." The waitress smiled at him and left them alone.

"You always start with three plates?" Oliver asked.

"Yeah. Dig in. It's all family-style here."

Oliver wondered how the man could have so much of an appetite. Half an hour ago they'd been looking at another man's corpse. And now that corpse was burning up in a fire his partner had set.

He wondered if Sally was eating right now, and if so, with

how much gusto. Probably a great deal, he thought. He doubted death and destruction bothered her that much. They might even turn her on.

"What are we going to do now?" Oliver asked.

"Wait for a while," Tyler said. "Eat. You really should eat something. Have a pot sticker."

"I don't want a pot sticker."

Tyler shrugged. "More for me." He popped one into his mouth. "It's good," he said, his mouth full.

Oliver sighed. "I still don't know who you people are," he said

Tyler ate another pot sticker. "We're private detectives," he answered.

"Oh," said Oliver. That was a much simpler answer than he had expected. "Really?"

"No," Tyler shook his head. "But close enough, I guess. Or I guess you could say we're a secret society, but there really aren't enough of us for that, I wouldn't think. How many people do you need before you can say you're a society?"

"I don't know," Oliver admitted.

"So why don't we say we're a group with a certain interest in...I don't know. I want to say *esoteric* things, but I'm not exactly sure what *esoteric* means."

"It means..." Oliver started to explain, but then he realized he wasn't positive either. "It means unusual, I think."

"Okay."

"Psychics and cyborgs."

"The cyborgs are gone," Tyler said. "And I don't know much about psychics, honestly. I've never met one, as far as I know. Artemis could explain it, but it's never really come up."

"Artemis. The little girl who isn't a little girl." Tyler nodded. "What is she, then?"

"A very old little girl," Tyler said.

"How old?" Oliver asked.

"I have no idea, honestly. I asked her once but she just looked at me like...well, I never asked again."

"Why does she look like a child?"

"I don't know." He shrugged. "She never hit puberty?" he guessed.

"I see," Oliver said, although he didn't see at all. "And you work for her. How did you get involved in this?"

"I used to be a cop," Tyler said. "Honolulu. I got mixed up in...well, that's not really important right now. When the smoke cleared, Artemis recruited me."

"And you just went along with her?"

"After what I'd seen?" Tyler asked. His eyes took on a faraway look for a moment. "She made an offer and I didn't have to think about it for long. I was never going to be the same person again." He used his chopsticks to toy with a piece of chicken. "I guess I could have buried my head in the sand and pretended none of it was real, but that's not me. I don't regret it, not really. My world is a lot bigger now. The things I've seen since then..." he trailed off.

"I've seen things you people wouldn't believe," Oliver quoted from an old sci-fi movie.

"You've got it," Tyler nodded. "That's it exactly."

"So there's you, and that psycho Sally…" A dark look crossed Tyler's face and Oliver knew immediately he'd gone too far.

"You want to cut her some slack," Tyler said, a little roughly. "She's had a bad time lately. The way she is right now, she's not always like that."

"What happened?" Oliver asked.

Tyler looked down, considering. "Something terrible," he said finally. "It's not my place to say. But the person you met today isn't the person I met two years ago."

It didn't seem worth pushing the issue. Oliver decided to change the subject. "So are you guys government agents? Some secret agency you could tell me about, but then you'd have to kill me?"

Tyler reached into his back pocket and found his wallet. He flipped it open and showed Oliver a badge that identified him as John Connor, a special agent with the FBI.

"Really?" Oliver asked. "Wait…*John Connor?*"

Tyler chuckled as he flipped the wallet shut. "No, of course not. Well, check that, the badge itself is real. If you run that through any government computer it'll verify my name and that I'm an agent, but it's not really true. I've never even been to Quantico. It's just part of the bag of tricks."

"How did you get the badge, then?"

"Artemis has contacts everywhere. I mean *everywhere*. And anything she can't get, Seven could probably make."

"You said that name before. 'Seven.' He's your tech

support guy?"

"Well, he's not just the guy who fixes the printer when it breaks, but yes. You may meet him, eventually, but he doesn't leave the office much. Has trouble with crowds."

Oliver nodded as if everything he was hearing did not sound completely nuts. "So it's just the four of you? That's just enough that you could all fit inside a van. You could drive around together, solving mysteries."

"I made that joke once," Tyler said. "Nobody else got it."

"Oh."

"And it's not just us. We actually have branch offices all over the world, but they're mostly just support staff with the odd specialist here and there. I doubt most of them have any idea what we actually do. Sally and I are the only field agents, at the moment. There are never more than a handful of us. Well, in my time, anyway. I can't say historically. Artemis has been doing this for a long time."

"How long?"

Tyler shook his head and shrugged. "Last chance for a pot sticker," he said, motioning at the soon-to-be-empty plate.

"That's okay," said Oliver.

"Your loss," Tyler said, popping it into his mouth.

The door to the restaurant swung open and a bedraggled homeless man wandered in. Oliver recognized him; he'd seen the man panhandling in the financial district dozens of times. He'd given the man change once or twice, if he remembered correctly. This place seemed pretty far out of his regular territory.

The man spotted Tyler and began shambling over to their table. "No, no!" the waitress tried to intercept him. "You leave! Bad smell!"

"It's okay, Li-Jen," Tyler called, waving her off. "He's with us. Hey, Oscar," he greeted the man. "You want to sit?"

Oscar stopped at their table but didn't sit. "This the guy?" he asked, looking Oliver up and down.

"Yeah."

"I know you," Oscar said.

"I work downtown," Oliver explained, a bit embarrassed. "Sometimes I give you…"

"You wear that awful tie sometimes," the man interrupted.

"What?"

"That green tie with the stripes," Oscar said, running his hand horizontally across his chest where a tie would have lain.

Oliver knew the one he meant. "That was my father's tie!" he objected.

"Let's leave it," Tyler said. "What do you have for us?"

Oscar looked back to Tyler. "Word on the street is it was a mistake," he said. "Wrong guy."

Oliver sighed. "I knew it." Of course it had been a mistake.

"How do you mean?" Tyler pressed. "Who had the contract out?"

"The lizards."

Tyler's eyes widened. "Holy shit, really?"

"Who are the lizards?" Oliver asked. It sounded like a gang

name from the 1950's, or the worst high school mascot ever.

"Never mind," Tyler told him. "What happened?" he asked Oscar.

"They had a prophecy," Oscar explained. "You know how the lizards get with that shit. I guess they figured out it wasn't *this* guy they wanted, because they just snatched some other dude off the street at Noriega and 35th. Cut his heart out and dumped him."

Oliver knew that intersection. It was only a few blocks away from his house. And someone had been *killed* there?

"So it's all off?" Tyler asked.

"They aren't out looking for him," Oscar said. "If they had people on the street we'd know about it."

"What about Mr. Teasdale?" Oliver asked.

"No word on him," Oscar said. He looked at Tyler questioningly. "Rocky's shop? He dead?"

"Yeah. We figure Teasdale went after him when the contract went bad."

"And the fire?"

"That was Sally."

"Oh. Figures. Well, that's all I've got for you. Your boy here's in the clear."

"Okay, thanks," Tyler said. "Hey, Oliver, give me a twenty?"

Oliver knew the drill this time. He went into this wallet and handed Tyler a twenty-dollar bill. Tyler handed it to Oscar.

"You could have just given it to me yourself," Oscar said to

Oliver.

"Yeah. I guess I could have," Oliver said.

"You want some *kung pao* to take with you?" Tyler asked.

"No, I ate already." He looked back to Oliver. "Don't wear that tie anymore. You want to wear solid colors."

"Oh," Oliver said. "Okay."

Oscar shambled to the door and was gone a moment later. Oliver looked back to Tyler. "So what now?" he asked.

"Now? I guess I take you home," Tyler said. "Looks like we're done."

"Who are the lizards?" Oliver wanted to know.

"It doesn't matter now," Tyler said. "The less you know about any of this the better, really." He leaned forward and waved his hands in an elaborate dance in front of Oliver's face. "This has all been a dream!" he intoned.

Oliver stared at him blankly. "I don't dream."

"Ah, it was worth a try," Tyler said. "Eat something. I'm going to report to Artemis and then I'll drive you back to your place."

Oliver looked at the empty plates that covered the table. Now he *was* feeling hungry, but the food was gone. "You ate everything already."

"Oh, well, that's easy to fix." He raised a hand to get the attention of the waitress. "Can we get some menus?" he called.

Oliver raised his eyebrows. "Menus? You're going to eat more?" The man had already put away enough food to feed a small family.

"I'd hate for you to eat alone," Tyler grinned. "See, you get a half day at work and a free dinner. This is turning out to be a good day for you after all!"

Chapter 10

They were a few blocks away from his house when Oliver said, "Maybe this *is* a dream. If it's my first one, how would I even know the difference?"

Tyler nodded thoughtfully. "I never thought about it like that. Well, if you're dreaming, maybe I am, too. Hey, did you ever see *Inception*?"

"Yeah," Oliver said. "I didn't get it at all."

"Me neither. But if you've never had a dream, I guess you wouldn't even know where to start. Huh. That *is* weird, never dreaming. I don't think I've ever heard of that before, and I've heard of a lot of things."

"It's just the way I am," Oliver shrugged. He didn't know how else to explain it.

Tyler had called Artemis as soon as they were back in his car and had briefly explained their situation. He listened to her for a moment, and then handed the phone to Oliver. "She wants to talk to you."

"I can't find any evidence that this was anything other than an error," the girl had said. Oliver still thought it was strange to hear a child talk so formally. "Nor can I come up with any reason you would be a target for assassination by anyone at all, let alone the Kalatari."

"The who?"

"Never mind that." He heard the girl sigh into the phone. "If you like, I am willing to place you in one of our safe houses for a few days, just to confirm that there is no further danger."

"But they got the guy they were looking for," Oliver said. "The lizards, or the *Kalatari*, whatever you call them. They killed someone out near my house."

"A man is dead. We have been able to confirm that."

"Then what's the problem?" Oliver found himself ashamed of the question the moment he asked it. A man was dead, after all, and here he was acting as if his own was the only life that was important. Could he be any more callous?

There was silence on the girl's end, and Oliver wondered if she had felt the same way and hung up on him. "This feels wrong," Artemis said finally. "While I have no evidence, I am certain that there is something unusual about you. The way you walk in the world is…" she trailed off. "I do not know. I feel as if I am witnessing the birth of something unique."

Oliver was quite certain he wasn't unique, but he did feel just a little bit flattered. Nevertheless, it was time to get back to his life. If he was back at his office tomorrow, he might be able to explain away the events of the day, although it would be a longshot. He was certain that any more time away would mean crossing the line permanently.

"I think I'd like to go home," Oliver said.

"Very well. Tyler will drive you."

"I don't mind getting a cab," Oliver offered.

"Tyler will drive you," the girl repeated, hanging up. And that was that.

Now he was nearly home and then this would all be over. Tomorrow he would go to the office and say…something. He didn't know what yet. He doubted he would be able to sleep tonight, so he'd have plenty of time to think about it.

Oliver sighed softly. As relieved as he was that he was no longer in danger, he couldn't help but feel the tiniest bit disappointed. This had been a wild, dangerous day, but he had to admit it had been an interesting break from his normal routine. He would probably not have another day like this in his lifetime. He wasn't entirely sure if that was a good or a bad thing.

Tyler drove the block around Oliver's house twice, looking carefully at each of the parked cars they passed. Nothing seemed amiss to Oliver. The neighborhood looked the way it always did. Did Tyler expect an assassin to be hiding in the bushes outside his house?

Finally, Tyler stopped the car. "Give me your keys," he said.

"What? Why?"

"I'm going to go inside and check it out. Just to make sure."

"I'm sure that's not necessary," Oliver said. "This is all over now."

Tyler shook his head. "Just trust me, all right? I'll be in and out in two minutes. Then you never have to see any of us again."

Oliver sighed again. Better safe than sorry, he supposed, and if it would make Tyler feel better... He was surprised to find he was beginning to like the man. "All right. It's kind of a mess in there, though. Sorry." Not having had guests over in ages, Oliver hadn't been especially strict about keeping his house clean.

"Doesn't matter to me," Tyler said. "I'm going to leave the car running. If I'm not back in five minutes, just drive away. Don't come looking for me. Artemis will find you." He got out of the car and shut the door quietly behind him. Oliver watched as he cautiously approached the house's front door, looked around carefully, and then put the key into the lock. Oliver had a sudden burst of fear that the house would explode as soon as Tyler opened the door, but it swung open the same way it had every other time someone had turned the knob. Tyler slipped inside the house, closing the door behind him.

Oliver shook his head softly. Had he really thought the house was going to explode? His life wasn't an action movie. At least not yet. But he had earned the right to be paranoid, hadn't he? Who could possibly blame him after an assassin had showed up at his office? That hadn't been a figment of his imagination, after all.

"Hey!" shouted a small voice from just outside the car. "Hey! Hey!"

Oliver looked around, startled. He hadn't seen anyone approaching the car, and even now he couldn't see anyone outside. Who was doing the yelling? Could one of his neighbors have the television on and a window open?

"Hey! Asshole!" The voice was insistent. "Down here, asshole!"

Oliver rolled down the car window. He still didn't see anybody, until he looked down and noticed a cat on the sidewalk looking up at him. It was Jeffrey, he realized. The cat he had kind of adopted, before he had run off. Jeffrey looked angry. "I've got a bone to pick with you," the cat said.

Oliver looked around, not sure how to begin this conversation, or if he should begin it at all. "Did you just talk?" he asked hesitantly.

"Of course I talked," the cat said, clearly annoyed. "What the hell did you do to me?"

"Me?" Oliver asked.

"This is your fault!"

On any other day, a cat calling him to the carpet would have been enough for Oliver to call a doctor and schedule a brain scan. But this wasn't any other day. He opened the door and stepped out of the car. Jeffrey backed away, watching him cautiously. "Don't try any more of your sorcery!" the cat warned.

"What? I'm not a sorcerer," Oliver said. He sighed and knelt down in front of the cat. "Look, I'm sorry," he said, his voice conciliatory. "I don't know what happened to you. It's been a weird day." That was certainly an understatement, Oliver thought. "Tyler can probably explain this."

"Who?"

"You probably saw him just now," Oliver said. "He went

into the house a minute ago. He knows about this stuff."

"I don't want to talk to him," the cat said. "He smells like a dog, and his shirt is ugly."

"He smells like a dog?" Oliver hadn't noticed anything unusual. Tyler smelled like anyone else, as far as he could tell. Not that he went around sniffing people, of course. The cat's sense of smell must be much more sensitive than his own.

"Anyway, I think he is busy with your other friends now," the cat continued, glancing up at Oliver's second-floor window. "So you better figure out what you did to me and put me back the way I was."

"I don't know how to..." Oliver stopped suddenly. "Wait, what other friends?"

"Your friends inside the house," the cat explained. "I saw them hiding in there earlier when I came looking for you. Two of them *stink*, by the way. Not like dogs. Way worse. You should really talk to them about it."

There were people hiding inside his house? Today wasn't Oliver's birthday, and even if it had been, he didn't have any friends who would be trying to throw him a surprise party. "Oh, crap," he said.

"What?"

Oliver looked back at his house. He needed to warn Tyler that he wasn't alone in there. He stood up and took a step toward the door, but suddenly the second-floor window shattered and a heavyset man came tumbling through it. He fell through the air, screaming, until he hit the ground with a sickening thud.

Oliver ran towards him intending to help, but stopped

short when he got a closer look. The back of the man's skull had been cracked open and Oliver could see blood and bits of bone on the pavement. The man was no longer breathing. This man, whoever he had been, was far beyond help.

Oliver could hear shouting coming from the other side of the broken window, followed by two gunshots and a cry of pain as a piece of furniture inside his house was smashed. Oliver saw Tyler struggling with another one of the intruders near the window. There was something strange about the other man's skin, Oliver thought. Tattoos? Tyler hadn't turned the interior lights on and it was difficult to see in the dark. No, they weren't tattoos. Maybe he had psoriasis or some other skin condition. A bad case, from the looks of things. The other man's skin looked as if it was covered in small, overlapping scales.

The new man spotted Oliver as he struggled with Tyler. "He's outside!" the man shouted to someone else. "Go!"

Tyler kneed the man violently in the groin and tossed him aside. "Get out of here!" he shouted down at Oliver. Then someone seized him from behind and dragged him out of Oliver's sight.

Jeffrey was at Oliver's feet, watching the fight above them with interest. "Use your magic," he urged Oliver.

"I'm not a damn sorcerer!" Oliver insisted.

"No? Then maybe you better start running," Jeffrey suggested.

Oliver heard more struggling from inside the house, another gunshot, and then a sickening crack. A long moment passed in silence, and then the front door opened and Tyler stepped outside. His Hawaiian shirt was badly torn and wet with blood. He had one hand pressed to his abdomen and was breathing heavily.

"Are you all right?" Oliver asked. It occurred to him at once that this was a stupid question. Of course the man wasn't all right.

"Sure," Tyler said, wincing. "No problem."

Oliver heard a screech of tires from down the street. A silver Miata was racing toward them. It pulled to a stop and Sally jumped out, silver pistols appearing in each hand.

"It's over," Tyler told her.

"How many?" she asked.

"Two lizards, three humans."

Oliver blinked. Tyler had just fought five people? At least one of whom had had a gun? And he'd *won*?

"They played us," Sally spat. "God damn it."

Oliver heard sirens approaching in the distance. "Thank god, the cops," he said.

Sally scowled at him. "You really want to explain this to the police?" she asked him, motioning with one pistol to the dead man lying on the pavement a few feet away.

"Lizards," Jeffrey said, looking up at the broken window. He sniffed the air. "That's it. That's why they smelled so strange to me. They're lizards that look like people."

Tyler and Sally stared at the cat in shock. "Oh yeah," Oliver said, realizing this part was new for them. "Guys, this is Jeffrey. Jeffrey, meet Tyler and Sally." It occurred to him that he was introducing them to a cat. Maybe he'd already seen the doctor and had that brain scan. Maybe he was in a hospital somewhere right now, and this was all some kind of fever dream.

"My name isn't actually Jeffrey," the cat pointed out. "But I'm not sure you could pronounce it."

"Wow," Tyler groaned, still wincing. "You really did make a cat talk."

"See?" the cat said to Oliver. "It's your fault. He gets it."

Oliver looked up the street. He could see flashing red lights now. In a moment the neighborhood would be swarming with police, maybe a SWAT team, and who knew what else.

"Is Seven on that?" Tyler asked.

"Yeah." Sally frowned, fingering one of her pistols. "Taking his damn time about it."

Oliver wondered what that meant, but it became clear when the sirens abruptly stopped and the flashing lights disappeared. Oliver saw car headlights turning away. Nobody was coming now. The street was quiet again.

"Huh," said Jeffrey. "Would you look at that?"

"I can't believe you have a talking cat," Sally said. "Artemis said there weren't any."

"There aren't," Jeffrey pointed out. "Cats can't talk. And I couldn't do it either, until this guy up and put the whammy on me!"

Tyler choked out a laugh. "Did you put the whammy on him?" he asked Oliver.

"No!" Oliver insisted.

"We can sort this out later," Sally said. "Right now…" she stopped as Tyler suddenly staggered forward, dropping to one knee. "T.?"

"Hey, he's bleeding!" said Jeffrey.

Sally bent down and ripped Tyler's Hawaiian shirt open. Oliver gasped. Tyler had two bullet holes in his abdomen and was bleeding profusely from them.

"Oh, shit," Oliver said.

"Yeah, don't worry about it," Tyler said. "It's not bad. I'll be fine."

"Dumbass," Sally said softly. "Why didn't you say you were hit? Can you stand?"

"Sure." Tyler strained for a moment but didn't move. "Well, no, actually."

"We've got to get him to a hospital," Oliver said.

"Or a vet," Jeffrey said. Oliver gave him a harsh look. "I told you he smells!" the cat complained.

Sally had a dark expression. "There's no time to take him anywhere," she said quietly. "He's bleeding out." She put a hand gently on the man's cheek. "T., I'm sorry. You've got to do it."

Tyler shook his head. "It's not that bad."

"You're not going to have a choice in a minute," she said solemnly. "You have a better shot to stay in control if you do it before it takes you."

Jeffrey tilted his head and sniffed the air curiously. He looked at Tyler. "You smell even worse now," he said.

"Yeah," Tyler nodded. "That happens."

"Hey," the cat said to Oliver. "I think we had better get out of here."

"We can't leave him," Oliver snapped.

"It's all right," Sally said to Tyler. "You're going to be okay."

"Fine," the other man conceded, gritting his teeth. "Get Oliver out of here. Touch base with Artemis when you're out of the city." His breaths were short and shallow now, and increasing in speed. "Get going. I don't think I've got much longer."

Sally squeezed his hand and then stood up. "Let's go," she said to Oliver.

"Are you serious?" Oliver asked. They couldn't abandon the man here.

Tyler suddenly screamed, doubling over in pain. Oliver saw him shudder, and his muscles seemed to ripple. Was he having a seizure?

Then there was a loud crack. Oliver gasped. One of Tyler's bones had just snapped. It was quickly followed by another.

"We have to go now," Sally said, urgency in her voice. "He can usually control himself, but he's in a lot of pain and I can't be sure."

"Go," Tyler urged through clenched teeth. Oliver stared at him in shock. Tyler's eyes had been blue when they had met this morning. Oliver was sure of that. But now the irises were yellow, and they seemed to glow as if they were being lit by a candle from somewhere deep inside his skull.

Oliver took a hesitant step back. He could hear more of Tyler's bones cracking horribly now, his limbs twisting around as if he were some kind of bizarre marionette. Oliver quickly realized that the bones were not simply breaking; they were reforming. Tyler was changing into something else.

"Yeah, let's go," Oliver said.

Sally and Oliver piled into the Miata. "Hey, wait!" Jeffrey yelled, jumping in after them. Sally put the car in gear and hit the accelerator. The tires screeched, and they pulled away from Oliver's house as if the car had been shot out of a cannon. In the passenger side mirror Oliver could see Tyler climbing to his feet in the street behind them, but the shape of his body was bizarrely different now. His upper body was like that of a bodybuilder, massive and muscled. His arms were longer than they had been before, reaching nearly to his knees. Oliver knew that they would end in sharp claws, and that he wasn't imagining the thick hair he thought he saw covering Tyler's shirtless torso. Tyler turned to watch them as the car sped away and Oliver could just barely make out the man's terrifying new face.

"He's a…" Oliver started. He knew the word he was looking for, but he wasn't sure he'd be able to say it. "He's…"

"He's a freaking werewolf!" Jeffrey cried out from the back seat. "Who the hell are you people?"

Sally turned the car north onto 19th Avenue. "Yes, he's a werewolf. Well, not really, but close enough. He doesn't flip out when there's a full moon or anything." She shrugged. "He *can* get a little testy, though."

"He's a werewolf? What are you, then?" Oliver asked. "Another werewolf?"

She glared at him. "Of course not."

"She smells weird, though," Jeffrey said. His little eyes widened. "She's a vampire! A dark fiend of the night!"

Sally glared at the cat in the rear view mirror. "I didn't teach him *that*," Oliver offered.

"I'm not a vampire," Sally told the cat. "Although that does give me an idea."

"What idea?" Oliver asked.

"Never mind. We're getting you out of the city." She looked at the cat. "I can't believe I'm saying this, but do you want to stay with us or go?" she asked the cat.

"I'm staying with him until he turns me back to normal," Jeffrey said.

"Whatever," Sally said. "But if you call me a 'dark fiend' again, little cat, I'm putting you through the window."

Jeffrey opened his mouth to say something, hesitated, and then shut it.

"Good call," Oliver said.

"Sorcerer," the cat muttered.

Chapter 11

Sally called Artemis just after they crossed over the Golden Gate Bridge. She stayed on the line long enough to tell the girl what had happened and where they had left Tyler. Oliver couldn't make out what Artemis was saying in response, but he could pick up enough of her tone of voice to tell the girl was not at all pleased.

Sally shook her head as she hung up the phone. "That went well."

"Is she mad?"

"As mad as she ever gets."

"I didn't realize she cared so much about what happens to me."

Sally shook her head. "It's more that she felt responsible for your safety after we intervened for you this morning. You were under her protection. And then she was fooled into thinking you were safe, when you were actually being set up. She's taking this personally now. That's lucky for you."

"Lucky?"

"Artemis is a good person to have on your side. She won't stop now until this is over, one way or the other."

That sounded a bit ominous to Oliver, but he decided to leave it alone. "So what are we going to do now?"

"Get you far away from here. Someplace safe."

"And that would be…"

"Stop talking now," Sally snapped. "I need to think."

Oliver shut his mouth. He didn't need to antagonize her. More questions could wait for a little while, when she seemed more receptive. But then again, she had yet to seem receptive to much of anything.

They drove in silence through Sausalito and then into San Rafael. Just north of the city Sally stopped for gas at a small Tesoro station. She went inside to pay with cash and returned with two bottles of diet soda. To Oliver's surprise, she offered him one. It was almost like a peace offering, he thought.

"I don't get anything?" Jeffrey asked.

Sally shrugged. "He's *your* cat," she said to Oliver.

"No, I'm not," Jeffrey corrected her. "You do get that cats aren't possessions, right? We're people, too." He paused. "That didn't sound right at all," he said thoughtfully. "Okay, not people, *per se*, but…"

"Enough," Sally said. "You're not his. Fine."

"Thanks," said Jeffrey. "Hey, can I borrow five bucks?" he asked Oliver. "I'll just go in there and buy myself a water, since nobody else here is going to do it. If anyone inside thinks that's unusual, I'll tell them to come out here and ask the sorcerer about it."

"I say we leave him here," Sally said to Oliver.

"No," Oliver said. "Whatever is going on with him, I'm starting to think I'm responsible for it."

"Damn right you are," Jeffrey said.

Oliver sighed. "Wait here." He went inside the store and bought a bottle of water and a set of cheap paper bowls. After a moment's thought, he picked up a package of ready-made tuna salad and crackers. Jeffrey probably wouldn't eat the crackers, but he might like the tuna.

Sally was hanging up her phone when Oliver returned. He was about to ask who she had been talking to when Jeffrey started dancing around his ankles.

"That's the stuff," Jeffrey said. "Hey, wait, is that fish?"

"Yes," Oliver said, feeling pleased with himself.

"Oh," the cat said.

Oliver paused. "You don't like fish? It's tuna."

"Fish is all right," said Jeffrey. "I like other things better, though."

Sally laughed. "Are you sure you don't want to leave him here?" she asked Oliver.

"What do you want to eat?" Oliver asked the cat.

"I like Thai food," Jeffrey said. "Those little spicy shrimps you get sometimes, those are nice."

"Well, I don't have any Thai food," said Oliver, beginning to feel exasperated. "Do you want the tuna or not?"

"I guess," said Jeffrey.

A few minutes later they were back on the freeway, Jeffrey sitting on Oliver's lap. Oliver was spreading spoonfuls of tuna salad on a cracker, which Jeffrey used as a kind of makeshift plate. If he didn't like tuna, the cat wasn't complaining now. He was eating with considerable enthusiasm.

Oliver decided this might be a good time to try his luck talking to Sally again. "You were going to tell me about the people who are after me," he began.

"No, I wasn't," Sally said.

"Please?" Oliver asked.

"Oh, come on," Jeffrey urged. "Throw the man a bone. He bought me tuna."

Sally sighed. "I don't know that much, to be honest. The Kalatari don't exist where I'm from."

"Where are you from?" Oliver asked. The way she had said that, Oliver got the idea that it must be quite some distance away.

Sally ignored the question. "They're humanoid, but reptilian. They share a common ancestor with humans a billion years ago or something."

"A billion years?" Oliver asked skeptically. "Before the dinosaurs?"

"Okay, not a billion years," Sally snapped. "You want the science of it, you have to ask someone else."

"It's all right," said Oliver. Nailing down the origin of the species wasn't the most important thing on the agenda right now.

"There aren't a lot of them left," Sally continued. "They killed off most of their breeding stock in their last civil war."

"That's depressing," Oliver said. "Isn't there anything they can do about that?"

"They've tried breeding with humans, but I don't think it's going well," Sally said casually. "Only a few of the offspring have survived, and none of the mothers, as far as I know."

"Who on earth would..." Oliver began to ask as Jeffrey retched.

"They have human servants," Sally explained. "You saw one of them. That dead guy on your sidewalk."

"They're servants? Like slaves?"

"No, followers would be a better word. They worship the Kalatari like gods, and do...whatever they're told, I guess. Errands, I don't know."

"That explains why you never see lizard people at Safeway," Jeffrey noted.

"Yes," Sally agreed.

"Or why they don't need jobs," the cat continued. "You'd think they'd have some trouble during the interview. 'Hi, I'm here about the job.' 'But aren't you a talking lizard?' 'Oh yeah, I forgot!'" The cat let out a high-pitched cackle, clearly amused with himself.

Sally looked over at him. "You done? That window opens, you know."

"He's done," said Oliver, giving the cat a warning glance. "So there are lizard people. Fine. I've seen weirder things today. What does any of this have to do with me?"

Sally shrugged. "No idea. They all take orders from a matriarch, who is also some kind of high priestess. What she wants with you I don't know. Artemis is working on it."

They continued north for another twenty minutes, until Sally eased the Miata onto Highway 37, which led due east. "Vallejo?" Oliver asked, trying to guess their destination. There wasn't much else in this direction.

"Sonoma," Sally said.

"What's in Sonoma?"

"A place that you'll be safe for a while."

"Which is?"

"Enough," Sally said. Question time was over, apparently.

They drove on in silence, eventually turning onto a narrow two-lane road that led them deep into wine country. Oliver had only been up here once before, on a company outing. They'd visited several small wineries in a minibus and Oliver had permitted himself to drink two entire glasses of wine, stopping immediately when he felt himself getting tipsy. He was worried he might say something foolish, like telling his department head that he thought the man was hopelessly incompetent and deserved to be fired ten times over. His department head, meanwhile, had gotten so drunk that he'd told one of the secretaries how much he looked forward to seeing her breasts every morning when he got to work. A week later the HR department decreed that all employees were now required to take mandatory sexual harassment training classes as part of a new policy. The employees were also told that the timing of the new policy's implementation was just a coincidence, completely unrelated to the very recent and sudden firing of

Oliver's former department head just after the company outing the week before.

After half an hour of driving through increasingly winding and treacherous roads, Sally turned onto a driveway that led to a tall, imposing metal gate. In the distance, Oliver could see a large white house that he probably would have described as a palatial mansion, if he had been a little more sure about what the word *palatial* meant.

A security guard in a dark suit stepped out of a small guardhouse, holding a clipboard at his side. He wore sunglasses in spite of the fact that it was dark out. Oliver could see that his clipboard had no paper or anything else attached to it. It was just for show, then? That seemed unusual.

Sally rolled down the window. "What do you want?" the guard asked coldly.

"I'm here to see your boss."

The man looked at the empty clipboard. "You aren't on the list."

"Even if there was a list I wouldn't be on it."

The security guard smirked at her. "Go away, little girl."

Sally looked at him curiously. "Do you know who I am?"

"Do I look like I…"

"Do you know who I am?" Sally repeated. There was no anger or arrogance in her voice, Oliver noted, but she spoke with a seriousness that commanded attention.

"Yes," the man admitted.

"Good. Now listen. Your boss owes my boss a favor. That

favor is being called in. Right now. Open up the gate, then call ahead and tell him I'm coming up." She smiled sweetly. "And then go ahead and call me 'little girl' again. But open the gate before you do. I don't want to waste my time looking for the switch in there when I'm done cleaning what's left of you off my jacket."

The man scowled, trying to stare her down. She held his gaze until he turned away and retreated into the guardhouse. A moment passed with nothing happening. Oliver wondered if the man was calling 911. But then the gate began to slide open. The man did not return.

"Punk ass," Sally muttered, starting up the driveway.

"That was…" Oliver began.

"Kinda scary," Jeffrey finished the sentence.

Sally shrugged. "He's more afraid of making his boss angry than he is of me."

"Who is his boss?"

"You're about to meet him."

Sally drove directly to the front of the house, ignoring an adjacent lot where several luxury vehicles were parked in a perfectly straight row. A man and a woman were waiting for them at the door. The man appeared to be in his mid-fifties, handsome, with salt and pepper hair. He was wearing a red smoking jacket and holding a half-empty wine glass. Oliver hadn't realized that people still wore smoking jackets. Unless they were Hugh Hefner, maybe.

The woman was another story. She was a Latina in her mid-twenties, with dark hair and eyes. She wore an immaculate dark blue business suit, which seemed bizarrely formal next to the man's casual attire. There was another obvious contrast; the man was smiling warmly at them, while the woman was expressionless, her eyes cold. She reminded Oliver of a snake coiled to strike. Or of Sally, for that matter.

The man looked oddly familiar to Oliver. Hadn't they met somewhere before? He was sure he knew the man.

Sally turned off the car and sighed. She took in the waiting pair for a moment. "Well, here goes," she said.

"You sound nervous," Oliver noted.

"I am nervous."

"I thought you said we'd be safe here?" Oliver pointed out.

"Yeah. It's kind of a gamble," Sally admitted. "I can't imagine he'd ever dare to cross Artemis, but you never know. Try not to make him angry. Or Maria."

"Maria?"

Sally nodded toward the sharply dressed woman. "His bodyguard. Or his attaché, maybe. Lover? I don't really understand their relationship, but she's probably more dangerous than he is." She reached over and scratched Jeffrey behind the ears, surprising Oliver and the cat both. "You stay here, little cat. All right?"

Jeffrey looked at the waiting man and woman curiously. "I think so," he said slowly. Oliver wondered what these people smelled like to the cat.

Sally opened her door and stepped out of the car, followed by Oliver a moment later. "My dear Sally," the man called warmly. He had a deep voice that was made for radio. "How are you?"

"Fine," Sally said. She turned to Oliver. "Oliver Jones, this is John…"

"You're John Blackwell!" Oliver interrupted, suddenly recognizing the man. They had never met before, but Oliver knew Blackwell by name and reputation. He had been on the cover of *Forbes* a few years ago.

"Indeed," he said, extending a hand for Oliver to shake. Oliver was stunned. John Blackwell was a legendary figure in the world of high finance. He ran a hedge fund with investments all over the world. He'd been an early investor in Google, along with several other firms that had grown into famous names. Oliver guessed he was worth somewhere around a billion dollars. He was also known to be something of an eccentric, Howard Hughes-esque figure, rarely leaving his estate.

Oliver understood at once why Sally had brought him here. This place was a virtual fortress, with armed security guards outside and who knew what else inside. It would be next to impossible for anyone hostile to get close to him.

"I know why you are here, of course," Blackwell continued. "It seems the lizards are quite eager to see the end of you, Mr. Jones. Filthy creatures," he sniffed, taking a sip of wine.

Oliver was stunned. John Blackwell knew about the Kalatari? What *else* did he know?

"You've spoken to Artemis, then?" Sally asked.

"Indeed," Blackwell said again. "I must say I'm surprised that she is intervening in this matter." He nodded at Oliver. "I take it he has some importance of which I am unaware?"

"Yes," Sally said. "It is very important to *Artemis* that he be unharmed." Oliver didn't miss her putting emphasis on the girl's name. Sally looked warningly at Maria, who simply stared back at her, her blank expression betraying nothing.

"Then unharmed he will remain," Blackwell smiled. "I receive so few visitors. Interesting ones, that is. I'm simply dying to get acquainted with you, Mr. Jones."

"I want your word that..." Sally began.

"You are on the verge of being rude," Blackwell cut her off sharply. "I have said he will remain unharmed, and so that is how it shall be." Blackwell turned and began to walk back to the house. Sally's hand moved an inch closer to her jacket pocket, where Oliver knew she had a pistol waiting. Oliver saw Maria shift her body weight almost imperceptibly. Waiting for Sally to make the first move, he thought.

"I'm fine," Oliver said to Sally. "But aren't you staying, too?"

Sally shook her head, relaxing only slightly. "I have to get back to the city. Find Tyler, if he's not back to himself yet. Then we're going to start hitting the Kalatari."

"Hit them?"

"That wasn't clear enough?" she asked. "We're going to fuck them up until they tell us what's really going on with you."

"Oh," Oliver said. He felt a little guilty. "It seems like...well, I should be helping you."

Sally started to smirk but stopped when she saw the earnest look in his eyes. "You really mean that, don't you?" she asked. "That's nice. But you've got a target on your back. We're not going to get anything done if you're tagging along."

"Sally, dear, are you staying or going?" Blackwell called over his shoulder.

"Going," she replied. She looked at Oliver. "Be good. Keep your hands to yourself in there and stay out of trouble. We'll be back for you."

"All right." Keep his hands to himself? He wasn't so awed by Blackwell's wealth that he was going to try to steal an ashtray or something.

"Come along, Mr. Jones," Blackwell said. Maria had stepped in front of her employer and was holding the front door open for him. "We'll be much more comfortable inside."

Oliver watched as Sally turned the car around and drove away. He could see Jeffrey looking at him from the back window. He almost expected the cat to wave to him. As soon as they were out of sight he turned and followed Blackwell past Maria into the house.

This wasn't such a bad situation, he thought. It wasn't like he got a chance to talk with someone in John Blackwell's position every day. The man was one of the shrewdest investors on the West Coast. With a little luck, he'd be able to convince the man to put some money into Western Pacific Capital. His bosses would forgive him nearly anything if he could bring in a new client with such deep pockets. In his line of work, making money was more important than a little indiscretion here or there. Nobody would ever mention the strange events that had taken place at his office ever again. Things were really looking up.

Maria closed the door behind them. She turned back to Oliver and smiled at him, revealing a pair of sharp fangs where her canine teeth should have been.

Oh, Oliver thought. Maybe things weren't looking up, after all.

Chapter 12

Blackwell caught Oliver staring at Maria's teeth. "Oh, don't mind that," he said dismissively. "She won't hurt you. Come along into the study." He paused. "Oh, dear, where are my manners? Would you care for a glass of wine?" He held up his own glass. "This is a rather cheeky Bordeaux, but my cellar is extensive, if you'd like something else."

Oliver was unable to take his eyes off of Maria, who looked back at him with barely concealed amusement. "Mr. Jones, it is rather rude to stare," Blackwell chided him. "Come now, this can't be the first time you have seen a vampire."

"It is, actually," Oliver admitted.

"Oh my, really?" Blackwell frowned. "How dreadful. What a dull life you must lead."

"I used to think so," said Oliver. Up until yesterday, it had been true. He was beginning to miss that dull life.

Another woman approached them, a busty redhead in a dark gothic dress which seemed to be made almost entirely out of gossamer lace. She carried a silver tray which held two glasses of red wine. Oliver couldn't help but notice the woman's unusually pale skin.

"Ah, yes," Blackwell said. "Thank you, Chantal." Blackwell drained the glass he'd been drinking from and placed it on the tray. He removed both of the new glasses and offered one to Oliver. "Please, Mr. Jones."

Oliver took the glass out of politeness. He was about to take a sip when a sudden thought occurred to him and he stopped, looking at the red liquid suspiciously. Blackwell laughed pleasantly and Oliver saw a small, evil smile on Maria's lips. "I assure you, Mr. Jones, it is merely wine," Blackwell said. "Well, I shouldn't say *merely*. It is very good wine. But it is only wine."

Oliver raised the glass again, sniffed at it, and then took a small, tentative sip. Wine. And an excellent wine, at that. Oliver was not a connoisseur. He'd always thought that people who described wine as "having a good nose" or "tasting of cherries and pine trees" were just bluffing in an attempt to impress others. But in this glass he could taste far more than simple fermented grape juice. He thought about the flavors as he swirled the wine around in his glass. Honey? Blackberries and…was that *chocolate*? Where could he get wine like this? And could he possibly afford it if he did find it?

"Excellent," Blackwell smiled. "Cheeky, wouldn't you say?"

"I don't know," Oliver admitted. "But it is very good."

"Prepare a room for our guest," Blackwell instructed Chantal, who turned and disappeared down the hall. Oliver watched as the pale woman left them.

"Is she a…" he began to ask.

"Oh, indeed," Blackwell said.

Oliver frowned. "So is that her uniform or something?"

"I do like the classics," Blackwell smiled, seeming just slightly embarrassed. "Not that I'm ever going to wear a cape, of course. That is an unfortunate stereotype."

Oliver nodded before he realized the implications of what the other man had just said. He looked at Blackwell in surprise. "You?"

"Of course," Blackwell said. He smiled widely and Oliver could see that he had fangs as well.

"Of course," Oliver sighed. Legendary hedge fund manager John Blackwell was a vampire. He lived in a big house with his vampire bodyguard and his vampire maid and…Oliver's eyes widened. "Is everyone here…" he began.

"I'm afraid so," Blackwell said, nodding. He noted Oliver's startled expression. "Never fear, my dear boy. Nobody will harm you. To do so would invite my punishment, and I'm afraid I am rather strict about that sort of thing. Come along. The study is this way."

Blackwell led Oliver into a magnificently appointed study that was nearly as big as Oliver's entire house. The furniture was early 20th century in style. If Oliver had seen it yesterday he'd have assumed it was all replica, but now he had to wonder if these were originals that Blackwell had collected over the years.

"Cigar?" Blackwell offered, sitting down.

"No, thank you," Oliver said.

"Just as well," Blackwell said. "They are terrible for you. That is of less importance to me, of course."

"Vampires don't get cancer?" That question had never occurred to Oliver before. Nor had it occurred to any rational person, ever, he thought.

"Of course not," Blackwell said, looking at Oliver like he was an idiot.

"Yeah," Oliver nodded, sipping his wine. It really was excellent. He wondered if Blackwell would offer him another glass.

"So," the other man said. "Tell me, Mr. Jones, why do the lizards want you dead?"

Oliver didn't know where to start. "I really don't know," he finally admitted. "This has been the craziest day of my life."

"You must have done something to upset them, did you not?"

"I'd never even seen one of them before tonight," Oliver said. "A...a *Kalatari*. I'd never even heard that word before. This time yesterday I wouldn't have believed they even existed."

"That must be frustrating for you," Blackwell noted sympathetically.

"I'm just a regular guy," Oliver said. "I'm a stock analyst. I look at spreadsheets. I write reports. The truth is I'm incredibly boring."

"I don't think that's boring," Blackwell said. "Analysis paid for everything you see in this house." Oliver saw Maria smirk. "Well," Blackwell said, catching her eye, "analysis, and just a bit of ruthlessness."

Oliver drank more of his wine, wanting to ask an obvious question but not wanting to sound foolish again. "You're a vampire," he finally said.

"Had we not established that already?" Blackwell asked.

"But that's wine you're drinking, isn't it?"

Blackwell peered at his glass curiously. "Why, I do believe it is," he said, as if he were realizing that for the first time.

"Shouldn't you be drinking...you know."

Blackwell raised his eyebrows. "Blood?"

"Yes."

"I *do* drink blood," Blackwell said, as if he were talking to a child. "I must do, don't I? Tell me, Mr. Jones, do you drink water?"

"Of course."

"Must you not drink water in order to live?"

"Yes."

"Do you drink *only* water?"

"No."

Blackwell raised his glass to Oliver. "Cheers." He took a drink.

Oliver wasn't sure that analogy would hold up to much scrutiny, but he got the point. "So this is..." he looked at Maria. "All these people are your vampire family, or something?"

"Or something," Blackwell replied. "We are not the

Munsters. A few of the staff here were already vampires who chose to serve me. The others were humans that I turned myself. As such, they are my subjects, and I am their master. Isn't that right, Maria?"

"Ever yours, my master," Maria said, tilting her head at him in an odd sideways nod.

Oliver was beginning to feel a bit tipsy. Had he had too much wine already? He really was a lightweight. "I find it safer to surround myself with those I know to be loyal," Blackwell continued. "Take Maria, here. She has been with me for…"

"One hundred ninety-eight years, my master." She seemed to be beaming, Oliver thought. He suspected her feelings for Blackwell went far beyond simple loyalty.

"Ah, yes." Blackwell swirled the wine in his glass, then drained it. "We will have to do something special for your two hundredth birthday," he said to her. "Think it over and let me know what you'd like."

What did vampires get for their birthdays, Oliver wondered. A victim with an unusual blood type? He wasn't sure he wanted to know.

"You really have no idea why the lizards want you?" Blackwell asked Oliver. He sounded disappointed.

"None. Really."

"Hmm. Well, they are despicable creatures. No sense of class at all. They really can't die out fast enough, if you ask me."

"Sally said something about that. They had a civil war?"

"Religious divisions would be a better way to put it. I don't know what they argue about, truly. Perhaps some think god has one tail, while others think he has three tails." Oliver saw Maria smirk again. "It hardly matters. They've slaughtered themselves out of a viable breeding stock. They have perhaps a hundred years left. After that they'll be a memory."

Not for most people, Oliver thought. But something had occurred to him. "You mentioned religion? We heard that they had killed someone else over a prophecy, but that turned out to be part of a trick to get me out of hiding."

"There could be some truth to that," Blackwell admitted. "Prophecy is something they take very seriously. I do find it unlikely that they would have a prophecy involving you, however. Prophecies about stock analysts must be fairly rare, I would think."

"Yeah." Oliver had to agree that that was probably true.

"And how do you know your new friends?" Blackwell asked. "You've met Artemis and Tyler, I'm sure. And of course poor Sally Rain."

"Poor Sally…" Oliver began to ask, but then decided he was more interested in a different question. "What exactly is Artemis? She looks like a little girl, but…"

"Exactly?" Blackwell asked. He shrugged. "I honestly don't know. I met her for the first time when I was very young. She was already old, even then. And by your standards, Mr. Jones, I myself am positively ancient."

"I'm almost afraid to ask," Oliver said. Any number of questions had occurred to him in the last few minutes. How much of what he had seen in the movies was true? Were vampires really immortal? Did they live forever, unless someone got lucky with a wooden stake? Did wooden stakes even work? What about sunlight and garlic?

"Then do not ask," Blackwell said. "Odd that they've taken you under their wing, though. Babysitting is not their usual line of work. Nor is it mine, but tonight will satisfy my most recent debt to Artemis." He leaned forward. "I am a man who pays my debts, Mr. Jones."

Oliver didn't care much for the idea that anyone was babysitting him, but he thought perhaps it was wise to show some discretion in a house full of vampires.

He was actually in a house full of honest-to-god vampires, he thought. This was real. How strange his life had become.

"Well, I don't think you have anything else to tell me right now," Blackwell said. "Another time I might like to talk a bit about the stock market. I enjoy hearing new opinions, and you seem at least passably intelligent. But it's late and I am growing tired." He smiled gently at Oliver. "And so are you, I'm afraid."

"Tired?" asked Oliver. He *was* getting tired; that was true. He had assumed it was the alcohol getting to him, but Blackwell's statement had made him wonder. "What is that, some kind of vampire mind trick?"

"Nothing so droll," Blackwell said. "Rather, it is the Seconal in your wine."

Oliver stared at his glass. He had nearly finished it. Fear gripped his heart like ice. Was this really happening again? Could he possibly meet someone who *didn't* try to drug him?

"Just relax, Mr. Jones," Blackwell said. "It's too late. It's impossible to fight it now."

Oliver tried to get to his feet, but only made it halfway up before collapsing back into his chair. The wine glass slipped out of his fingers. He expected it to shatter on the floor, but in the span of a heartbeat Maria was on one knee next to him, the glass clutched safely in her hand. Even through the fog that was quickly overtaking his mind, Oliver managed to be astonished. He had never even seen the woman move.

"Thank you, my dear," Blackwell said. Maria rose and nodded at him, placing the glass delicately on a nearby table. "Do forgive my own rudeness, Mr. Jones. I gave my word you would not be harmed, and so you will not be. But neither can I have you wandering around my estate, taking note of my affairs. There is a great deal here I simply cannot afford to let you see."

Oliver wanted to reply that he couldn't care less about Blackwell's secrets; all he wanted to do was to stay alive. But all he could manage to say was, "Don't care."

"I'm sure you don't," Blackwell smiled. "Maria will show you to one of the guest bedrooms. Well, I suppose she will have to *carry* you to one of the guest bedrooms. Don't be concerned about her; she is quite capable. In the morning, perhaps you will be so good as to join me for breakfast. We're having an Italian." He looked at Oliver expectantly.

Oliver tried to speak, but he could no longer find the energy to make his lips move. "That was a joke, Mr. Jones," Blackwell explained. "You see, I implied that we would be eating an Italian *person*." He regarded Oliver with disappointment. "That was funny, wasn't it, Maria?" he asked her.

"Very funny, my master."

Blackwell sighed. "She would say that anyway," he said to Oliver. "All these years, and I'm not sure I ever developed a sense of humor. Maria, be a dear and help Mr. Jones to his bed."

Maria bent down and wrapped her arms around Oliver, then lifted him up as easily as she might have a child, draping his head carefully on her shoulder. Oliver found he could no longer keep his eyes open. "Ssh," Maria whispered. "That's it. Go to sleep." Her voice was calm and soothing, like a mother's, but her breath was cold on his neck. Oliver wanted to scream, but he knew he was too far gone. He felt himself drifting off as she began to carry him away, and then everything was lost in comforting blackness.

Chapter 13

Oliver had been staring up at the lacy white canopy of a four-poster bed for several minutes, his vision lazily drifting in and out of focus, before his mind managed to fully register that he had woken up. He felt dizzy and nauseous, as if he'd taken a serious blow to the head and was dealing with the aftereffects of a concussion. Had someone hit him? Not that he could recall, but he had been drugged into unconsciousness twice within a twenty-four hour period, and he'd had a nice glass of wine to top that off. Who could tell what all of that was doing to his system?

He still didn't know what Sally had sprayed him with back at his office, but Blackwell claimed to have put Seconal in his wine, which was a drug Oliver had at least heard of before. Wasn't it used to knock people out before surgery? It was a barbiturate, if he remembered correctly. He was sure that mixing barbiturates, alcohol, and whatever else he'd been given was a very bad idea. It might be a good idea to see a doctor when all of this was over.

Oliver was still very tired, but he wasn't sure he wanted to go back to sleep. He wasn't even sure he knew *how* to go to sleep naturally anymore. Maybe he'd have to ask someone to come in and knock him out. Wasn't that what had happened with Michael Jackson?

For a moment Oliver wondered if all of this could simply be his first ever dream. Everything from the time he had supposedly woken up yesterday morning until now. He had no experience of what dreams were like, so how could he really say it wasn't?

Or maybe this was all a hoax. An incredibly elaborate, disturbing hoax, but one could make a case that nothing as bizarre as recent events could possibly be real. He certainly wouldn't believe this story if someone else was telling it to him.

Was *Candid Camera* still on the air? Oliver wasn't sure. He hadn't seen it in years. What would Allen Funt be saying right now? "We've convinced this man that he's in a house full of vampires. Let's watch what happens!"

Allen Funt was dead, wasn't he? Maybe he wasn't, and that was part of the prank, too.

Oliver sat up slowly, but not slowly enough to keep his head from spinning. He shut his eyes and tried to wait it out. After a moment things seemed to slow down again. Oliver decided that there was no way he'd be joining John Blackwell for breakfast. Maybe he'd just wait outside the house until someone came and picked him up. Or maybe he'd take a cab out of here. He just wanted to get away from this.

Oliver looked around the room, moving his head slowly in an attempt to prevent another dizzy spell. The bedroom was fairly Spartan for a man of Blackwell's means. The queen-size bed itself was elegant enough; Oliver couldn't recall ever seeing a four-poster bed complete with a canopy in his life, but other than that the room held only a bedside table and an oak dresser in one corner. There was no television, no artwork, nothing that would have made anyone call the room comfortable. Blackwell must not care to have long-term guests, Oliver thought. Nobody would ever make themselves feel at home here.

Or perhaps this room belonged to one of his "subjects." That was the word he had used, wasn't it? He wondered what it meant for a vampire to have subjects. Did they receive a salary? Would *slave* have been a better word?

The room had only one door. Oliver assumed it must lead to a hallway. He hoped he wouldn't have a need to go find a bathroom later. Even with Blackwell's assurance that nobody here would dare harm him, he was fully aware that to a house full of vampires, he must look like a hamburger with legs.

A digital clock on the bedside table read 2:52 am. He'd only been asleep for a few hours, then. He had no idea what dose of drugs he'd been given, but it seemed apparent that Blackwell had just wanted him out of the way for a while. It clearly hadn't been an attempt to hurt or kill him. He shouldn't be in danger here.

It occurred to him how absurd that statement would sound to any rational person. He was alone in a secluded, heavily guarded house in the country, and everyone in said house other than him was a vampire. Not teenagers dressing up in black clothes and wearing too much eye makeup. Real, honest-to-god vampires. He was *definitely* in danger here.

Oliver lay back in the bed and closed his eyes. He supposed

he should try to get some more rest. There was no telling what tomorrow would bring, but he felt confident that nothing else would be happening tonight.

There was a soft *click* at the door. Oliver sighed and opened his eyes. Why couldn't anything work out the way he hoped?

He sat up again, shutting his eyes as another dizzy spell hit him. There was more nausea, as well. For a moment he was sure he was about to vomit, but the feeling quickly passed. He opened his eyes in time to watch the door slowly open. The maid he'd seen earlier, if that was really her job description, slipped into the room silently. She was still wearing her lacy black dress. She smiled at Oliver and shut the door quietly behind her.

What had her name been? Something that sounded like a brand of champagne. "Chantal," Oliver said, remembering. "Um…hello?"

She smiled at him again and Oliver could see her fangs glistening across the darkened room. They were eerily bright. "You remember my name," she said. "I'm flattered, Mr. Jones."

Oliver assumed she had been sent to check on him. "I don't need anything right now," he said, just a bit nervously. "Do you happen to know if anyone called here asking about me? Artemis, maybe? Or Tyler?"

"No," Chantal said. She took a step closer to the bed. Oliver saw something in her eyes he didn't like. It was hunger, mixed with a dollop of lust. It was a look he didn't enjoy being on the other end of.

"Ah, okay. Well, thanks for dropping by," Oliver said. He

heard a small tremble in his voice and hoped she hadn't noticed it.

Chantal sighed. "Mr. Jones, I'm afraid I need something from you." She stopped at the edge of the bed, close enough to reach out and touch him if she'd wanted to.

"Oh, really?" He smiled, attempting to look calm. "What is it?"

She suddenly climbed onto the bed with him. "It's something only you can give me," she said.

This was a cliché, Oliver thought. Wasn't this directly out of Bram Stoker? The sexy vampire woman was going to try to seduce him now? There had to be a way to head this off. "Your dress is getting wrinkled," Oliver pointed out. Then he blinked in surprise at himself. Was that really the best he could come up with?

"I've been waiting so long," Chantal breathed.

Oliver wondered how far he'd get if he tried to run, or if he would even make it to the door in his current condition. But then he remembered how fast Maria had moved earlier. If that speed was typical of vampires, he wouldn't have had a chance, even on his best day. Much less when he was fighting the effects of narcotics.

Chantal pushed him roughly back onto the bed and threw one leg over his hips, straddling him. In another context, and with a *living* woman, Oliver might have found himself quite turned on. At the moment, though, all he could think about was keeping his blood inside his body.

She leaned down and caressed his cheek with her hand. "Handsome boy," she said.

"Thank you," he replied automatically. "You're very…" he began to say, before he caught himself. Politeness had a time and a place, and this was neither. "Mr. Blackwell said I'd be safe here." He heard fear in his own voice and hated himself for it.

"Yes, he did." She leaned down and licked his cheek like a puppy might have. "I suppose he's going to be very angry with me," she breathed.

"Definitely. Definitely very angry," Oliver said. Good god, he was actually aroused, he suddenly realized.

"I guess you'll just have to kill him for me," Chantal continued.

Oliver blinked. That wasn't what he had been expecting at all. He had thought all she wanted was a late-night snack. "Excuse me?"

"I'm going to make you mine," she said. "And then you'll kill him for me." She stroked his other cheek, seizing his wrist when he tried to stop her. Her grip was like a vice. "No," she said sternly. "Don't try to fight me. You're nowhere near strong enough, and I don't want you damaged."

"Please don't," Oliver said simply. He knew there was nothing else he could do now except beg.

"It's okay," she said soothingly. "It's not going to hurt." She frowned suddenly. "Well, that was a lie. It *is* going to hurt. A lot. But you'll get over it."

"I don't understand," Oliver said.

She leaned down again and brushed her lips gently across his cheek. "I want to be free," she said into his ear. "Once I've turned you, you'll be under my control. For a little while, at least, you'll be compelled to do whatever I command." She smiled. "He won't see you coming until it's too late. So you'll kill him for me, and then my bondage will be over." She shrugged. "Or you might fail, but you'll be dead and he'll never know which of us turned you. There are more likely suspects than me." She kissed him again. "My *dear* man, I've waited so long for this chance."

"What about Maria?"

"Oh, she'll definitely kill you," Chantal said. "Although I suppose if you did manage to beat her somehow, you would be my first subject." She smiled. "Either way I can't lose."

Chantal placed her hands around Oliver's upper arms and gripped him tightly. "Don't struggle now," she whispered. She leaned forward and kissed him delicately on the neck. A second, almost sensual kiss followed, and then she opened her mouth and bit into him.

Oliver felt her sharp fangs penetrate the flesh of his neck deeply. The pain was like being burned with a pair of fiery needles, so hot he wondered if the wound would smolder when she let go of him. He tried to scream, but no sound would come out of his mouth other than a high-pitched wheeze. He felt Chantal's fangs retract, her lips pressed tightly around the wound. His blood spurted into her mouth and she began to drink.

After a few swallows she pulled back and looked at him curiously, wiping his blood off of her bottom lip. "You taste funny," she said, a mischievous glint in her eye. "Must be the drugs I put in your wine. Sorry about that."

Oliver was breathing hard. "Jesus, that hurt," he groaned.

"Oh," she said sympathetically. "My dear boy, that wasn't the painful part."

Chantal extended an index finger and carefully traced a line across her left breast with the fingernail, leaving a narrow red trail in its wake. Blood began to trickle down her chest, at first only a few drops, but then more as the wound began to open. She leaned down and pulled Oliver up into a sitting position, then put her hands delicately around the back of his head. Slowly she guided his head down to her breast, as if helping a baby to nurse. "Drink," she said, pressing his lips against her bleeding skin.

Oliver wanted nothing more than to keep his mouth tightly shut, but the combination of drugs and the bleeding wound in his neck had left him weak and without the will to fight. And there was something about the smell of the woman's blood that was beginning to appeal to him. It would be sweet and spicy, he knew. He found that he wanted it. Something was changing inside of him, making him want to drink it.

Chantal stroked the back of his head gently, but didn't release her grip. "Go ahead," she said. Oliver's lips were wet with her blood now and he could taste her. Instead of metallic bitterness, he tasted something wonderful. It was as sweet as he had imagined, but it was also so much more. It was as if someone had bottled the taste of sex. He wanted more now; he wanted to drink it in deeply.

Oliver's lips parted and her blood entered his mouth. He drew it in and swallowed. It was perfect, but it wasn't enough. He wanted to do this forever. He swallowed again, savoring the blood as it went down his throat. But the blood still wasn't coming fast enough to satisfy him. He needed to open her. Oliver hesitated only for a moment, then he pressed forward and bit into her flesh.

Chantal pulled back, a bemused look on her face. "My goodness, you are a hungry boy," she said.

Oliver swallowed again and again. Chantal let him drink for a moment longer and then finally pushed him away. "I think you've had enough," she said with a smile. She sighed deeply. "Was that good?" she asked him.

"More," Oliver said.

"Not yet," she said. "Later you can have all you want. But for now," she frowned. "You see, *this* is the painful part."

Oliver looked at her in confusion. What did she mean? That hadn't hurt at all. He looked at the wound on her breast, which was already beginning to close. Could that have been what she meant?

He felt his stomach turn over and he was suddenly nauseous again. It was much worse this time than it had been before. Blood didn't agree with him at all, apparently.

Then the pain hit him, and Oliver screamed.

It felt as if he had swallowed a handful of burning razor blades and they were tearing his insides apart. His body convulsed violently and he screamed again. Chantal frowned at him. "Not so loud, please," she chided him. She pushed him down hard and pressed a palm against his mouth, clearly meaning to stifle the noise. "It doesn't last long," she said reassuringly.

Oliver panicked. This was all wrong, he thought. All of this. How could blood ever have appealed to him? How had she made him want to drink it? It must be part of how vampires feed, he thought. Some kind of seduction.

He could feel her blood hot in his veins now. It was running through his body, radiating heat down to the ends of his fingers and toes. He could feel something changing in his body. In a short time he'd be one of them, he knew. It was too late for him.

No, he thought. This wasn't going to happen. This *couldn't* happen.

"There, there now," Chantal cooed. She didn't remove her hand from his mouth. "You're almost there."

No, he wasn't, Oliver thought. It couldn't possibly happen. Vampires weren't real. In spite of the fact that he was looking at one, he suddenly felt certain that this wasn't really happening. It was a dream. He was having his first dream. He wasn't really turning into a vampire.

Oliver heard a sound like rushing water in his ears. The noise built until it was loud enough to drown out everything else in the room. There was something familiar about it, he thought. Hadn't he heard this same noise before, and not so long ago?

Then the room around him began to move. At first it was minute, as if he'd looked away for a moment and when he looked back everything around him had shifted slightly. Then his vision blurred. Chantal was still there, but she was now a nearly formless blob above him. The room behind her spun around them.

Oliver's vision focused on Chantal again but the room was still moving. Chantal looked down at him curiously. "What is it?" she asked.

And then everything stopped moving, instantly snapping

back into place. The sound of rushing water was gone. The room was still there, just as it had been a few moments ago. Chantal was smiling down at him, hand still pressed over his mouth.

Oliver felt one more jolt of pain, and then he caught fire.

Chantal screamed in terror and scuttled backwards, falling off the end of the bed to the floor. Oliver sat up and looked at his arms. He was covered in flames. But while he could feel heat, the flames weren't burning him. His clothes and the bed he had been lying on were unscathed.

Oliver climbed to his knees. The razor blades in his stomach were gone. There was only fire now. Cleansing fire. *Of course*, he realized. That was the purpose of the fire. It made perfect sense to him now. The fire was there to burn the vampire blood out of him.

That made sense, didn't it?

Oliver leaned forward and vomited. He saw bits of Chinese food and the blood he had just consumed leave his body and splatter on the mattress. Incredibly, the blood itself appeared to be boiling. Rather than being absorbed into the sheets and mattress, he saw the blood sizzle and evaporate like water landing on a hot frying pan.

Chantal was on her feet, backing away from him towards the door. Her eyes were wide. "What are you?" she screamed at him.

Then the bedroom door burst open, tearing itself off its hinges and crashing to the floor. Maria stood in the doorway, still wearing her immaculate business suit. Oliver could see John Blackwell a step behind her, along with two other people

Oliver could only assume were more vampires.

Blackwell stared at Oliver. "What on earth?" he asked in wonder. Maria looked over her shoulder at him questioningly. She wouldn't make a move without instructions, Oliver knew, but she'd do whatever her master commanded.

It was time to get out of here, Oliver thought. He couldn't trust any of them. How long would it be before another one of them tried to make a meal out of him, or use him for their own purposes? He wasn't safe here.

Even with his body on fire he wasn't sure he could get past the vampires. What should he do?

He needed a door, but the room's only exit was blocked. But if there had been another door, he could use it. He needed another door. A door that led somewhere else. Somewhere far from here.

Why did the bedroom have just one door? He needed it to have another one.

He heard rushing water and the world shifted yet again. When it snapped back into place Oliver suddenly saw the room's other door. In his panic he had somehow not noticed it before, but there was a door just behind him. He stepped toward it hesitantly. How had he not noticed it when he had woken up earlier? He had been so sure there had been only one door.

"Where the hell did that come from?" asked one of the vampires, staring at the new door in shock.

"Master?" Maria asked, looking at Blackwell. She was nervous, Oliver thought. Why was she nervous? Oliver took another step toward the new door.

"No!" Blackwell cried, throwing a hand forward. "Mr. Jones, please wait!"

"He's a sorcerer!" said one of the other vampires.

"No," Oliver said, but his voice sounded very strange to him. It was deep and echoed strangely, as if he were shouting up at them from the bottom of a well. "I'm not."

He turned to the door. It hadn't been there before, had it? No. But that hardly mattered now. It was here, and it would take him away. He turned the handle and opened it. He could see nothing on the other side, but the door frame itself was filled top to bottom with what looked like shimmering blue water. The door wasn't a door from one side of a wall to another, he realized. It was a door from one place to another place. *Of course*, he thought. That made perfect sense. *Didn't it?*

But where did this door go? It hardly mattered, Oliver thought, as long as it led to someplace safe. Somewhere far from this house of vampires.

Oliver raised a hand and touched the shimmering blue water. It yielded to his hand, and he saw his fingers disappear into it. He pulled his hand back and his fingers came with it. He wiggled them curiously.

"Stop him," commanded Blackwell. Oliver saw Maria shift her body weight but he could see things now he hadn't been conscious of before. He could see the path she would take to get to him. She was never going to have the chance, he thought. Oliver shut his eyes and stepped forward through the new doorway. He was going somewhere safe.

Oliver opened his eyes but all he could see was blue light, so bright he had to close his eyes again. Strong winds buffeted his body this way and that, as if he had stepped directly into the path of a hurricane. Then as suddenly as it had come, the wind was gone. Everything was calm again.

Oliver opened his eyes. He was outdoors now, standing on dirt path surrounded by pine trees. A short distance away he could see a small pond with benches and picnic tables nearby. A park, then?

Oliver looked behind him. There was no door there, and nothing to suggest he hadn't simply walked here from somewhere else.

He held up one hand. He was no longer on fire. That was a relief.

The sun was beginning to come up on the horizon. Oliver stared at it in wonder. It had been dark out when he had woken up in Blackwell's house, and it would have stayed that way for hours yet. But it was morning here. How much time had passed? Was it even the same day?

For a moment he wondered if he really had been turned into a vampire. Would the sunlight kill him? But the sun's rays felt good, warm on his skin. If sunlight killed vampires, he could be fairly certain he was not one.

With nothing better to do, Oliver began walking up the path. Before long it forked. A broken old wooden sign stood there to give directions. He read it and at first wasn't sure what to make of it. According to the sign, to the left was the butterfly kingdom, and to the right were the chimpanzees and the lions.

Oliver suddenly knew exactly where he was. No time had passed at all, he realized. The sun was coming up because he was on the other side of the country. He was in Maine.

He wondered if people ever fainted in real life, or if that was something that only happened in the movies. Because this would have been a great time for it.

Chapter 14

Oliver had to stop for a moment and shake off another bout of dizziness. Of all the insane things that had happened to him in the last twenty-four hours, he almost found this one the hardest to believe. Five minutes ago he had been in a bedroom in California, surrounded by vampires. Then he'd walked through a door that hadn't been there only a moment before, and now he was at Binkle's Roadside Zoo and Amusements. In Maine. If he remembered correctly, it was about an hour's drive from Portland, not far from the coast. And the Atlantic Ocean, not the Pacific he saw nearly every day.

Oliver had been here once before, many years ago, when he was still a small child. His parents had taken him to the Maine coast for a vacation. They'd stopped in countless small towns for "antiquing," which his mother had developed an instant passion for. Oliver remembered that he had eaten lobster for the first time on that trip. He'd been reluctant, believing that their large red bodies looked suspiciously like giant cockroaches, but his father had insisted, telling him that they were a delicacy, and one he had just spent a great deal of money on at that.

And on one of their drives through the country his father had brought them to Binkle's, which boasted one of the tallest Ferris wheels in the state and a small but diverse menagerie, which included lions. "Straight from the African jungle!" Oliver's father had told him. He'd read it on a billboard he'd spotted on the freeway.

The zoo did have two lions, but they had been rescued from a private collection in Milwaukee and had never seen the jungle. They regarded the passing throng of tourists with a certain degree of boredom, having learned some time ago that they couldn't scale the walls of their enclosure in order to snatch a quick snack. Oliver had been terrified of them nonetheless, certain that the lions would find a way to escape and eat him. His father had picked him up and held him close, telling him in a soft voice that this was a safe place. There was no danger here.

Oliver laughed now. It made sense, in a perverse kind of way. He had felt safe here, all those years ago, and safety had been the only thing on his mind back when he'd wanted to escape from the vampires. He'd wanted to be safe somewhere far away. Now he was clear on the other side of the country. Next time he'd have to try to wish he could be safe somewhere closer to home.

That answered the *why*, then, but not the *how* part of what he was doing here. How had he done it? Maybe Jeffrey had been right. Was he a sorcerer? For that matter, was a sorcerer something that a person could be? Maybe there was a book or something he could look at.

Binkle's had been closed for years, Oliver knew. He'd seen

a blurb on the news some time ago. It had fallen on hard times and the animals had all been shipped off to other zoos. He wasn't sure what had happened to the lions. Would they be able to speak to him now, if he wished for it hard enough? That would make as much sense as anything else that was happening in his life.

He should probably get out of here, he thought. He doubted there were any security guards on the grounds, but an abandoned roadside zoo could not possibly be the best place in the world for him.

Oliver started walking along the path, looking around for an exit sign. After a moment he spotted one and headed in that direction. As he had suspected would be the case, no security guards came running to intercept him. He found the dilapidated condition of the place more than a little depressing. This had been a good memory. He hoped somebody would buy the place and fix it up. He wasn't a fan of roadside zoos, but it wouldn't take much to turn it into a passable amusement park. You could put in a few rides for the kids, sell popcorn and candy. It would be nice.

Oliver stopped suddenly and looked around. He was almost surprised that none of the things he had just envisioned had magically appeared before his eyes. Lately it seemed that anything he thought about wound up happening somehow.

Was there any chance of that actually working? Oliver looked around to double-check that nobody was nearby, and then he said aloud, "I want popcorn."

No popcorn appeared. Maybe he was doing it wrong? "I wish for popcorn," Oliver said. Nothing. "Abracadabra. Hocus Pocus." He wiggled his fingers in the air as if he were casting a magic spell.

Still nothing happened. Oliver sighed. He felt foolish, but he was actually a little relieved. There was nothing wrong with him. There must be another explanation for all of this, however bizarre it would turn out to be.

Maybe he needed a physics textbook. Something very advanced, and probably theoretical.

After a few minutes he came to the main gate and stepped through a rusty old turnstile, exiting the park. The parking lot was devoid of cars, its pavement cracked and strewn with litter.

Should he call a cab? Oliver spotted a bank of three pay phones near the park's ticket booth. This place really had been closed a long time, he thought. He couldn't remember the last time he'd seen a pay phone. He'd have to remember to buy a prepaid cell phone the next time he was at a 7-11. He felt naked without one.

Oliver checked the pay phones but was not surprised to find that two of them had been vandalized to the point of destruction, and the other had no dial tone. There would be no cab for now, then. He'd have to walk.

Oliver walked to the edge of the highway and looked to the left and the right. No cars were coming from either direction. But it was still early, and who knew how much traffic this road got, anyway? Oliver searched his memories. He was sure that Portland was the nearest large city; he could recall eating dinner with his parents on board an old ship that had been converted into a restaurant the night before they'd been to the zoo. But which way was it? Was anything else nearby, ideally much closer? As much as he tried, he couldn't come up with anything. He'd spent much of the driving portions of that trip absorbed in a book about elves and dragons. If he were lucky, he would not run into either of those things during his walk.

Oliver looked back at the zoo. For a moment he entertained the thought of staying there. He could go inside there and hide for days, maybe. It seemed like the last place anybody would be looking for him. What were the odds that scheming vampires and evil lizard people were going to track him down out here?

But food and water would become a serious issue, he realized. He'd never eaten his lunch and hadn't kept his dinner down, and his stomach was already rumbling. It was time to get going.

Which way to go, though? It hardly seemed to matter. He thought about flipping a coin but realized he didn't have one, so after a moment's hesitation he turned to his left and began walking down the highway. The road seemed to angle downward in that direction, which would make the walking easier. And Portland was at sea level, he remembered. That couldn't possibly be the closest he was to *some* kind of civilization, but if it was, he could at least hope he was going in the right direction.

Oliver walked. The sun was rising through the trees and he was beginning to feel warm. That was something to be thankful for. He didn't have a jacket. Maybe he could pick one up when he found a cell phone. And if he was lucky, maybe he could buy a gun. He had no idea what firearms laws were like in Maine but if he could get a pistol, at least he'd feel a little safer.

As the sun continued to rise Oliver began to hear birds chirping in the trees. It was a good sound, he thought. At least that was a little bit of normalcy. Lately there hadn't been much of that to go around.

Still, he did have to think he'd handled recent events fairly well. He had managed to get through all of it without crying or wetting his pants. He could take some small pride in that. Certainly some people would have ended up in the nuthouse if they'd had a day like his.

Not for the first time, Oliver paused long enough to wonder if that had already taken place. What if he was strapped to a hospital bed somewhere and this had all been a delusion? In a lot of ways that made more sense than what was happening now.

He was wondering if there was a way to test that theory when he heard a vehicle approaching from behind him. He turned and saw a pickup truck heading in his direction, slowing down as it came closer. Not sure of the protocol, Oliver put his fist out and stuck his thumb in the air. That was how people hitchhiked, wasn't it? He'd only seen it before on television. Nobody hitchhiked in San Francisco. You'd have to be suicidal to try it there.

The truck stopped and a jovial man shouted to him from the driver's seat, "Where you headed?"

"Portland," Oliver said.

"Portland? Well, it's gonna take a while. You're going the wrong way."

Oliver sighed. Of course he was. "Well, what's *this* way?" he asked.

"New Hampshire," the man said. He looked at Oliver suspiciously. "You been drinking there?"

"I'm thinking about it," Oliver said truthfully.

"You want a lift?"

"Where are you going?"

"Boston. I don't mind the company, if you got some gas money. I can drop you off somewhere along the way, if you want."

Oliver felt for his wallet. It was still tucked away in his back pocket. At least that was one thing he wouldn't have to replace. "Sure. Why not?"

The man leaned over to unlock the passenger door and Oliver climbed in. He had never hitchhiked in his life and would never have considered doing so before now, but what was the worst that could happen? The man could turn out to be a murderer or some kind of sex pervert, but those things seemed fairly mundane now, compared to what he'd been dealing with lately. He might even find them boring, he realized.

"Name's Smith," the man said, extending a hand.

Oliver shook it. "I'm Sam," he lied. On any other day he would have felt awkward about the lie, but now he found it no longer bothered him. He might even be doing the guy a favor, if anyone questioned him about it later.

"Good to know you, Sam. All right, let's go." Smith put the car in gear and they started off down the road. Oliver was grateful for the ride. Once they got to a city he'd be back in his element. He'd be back in the world of taxis and hotels. And airports. Airports were good. He could buy a ticket to somewhere far away from here. Magic doors were overrated.

Smith had been listening to an oldies station on the radio.

He turned it down. "So where you from, Sam?"

"Washington," Oliver said. That was true. "Little town near Spokane you never heard of."

"You miss it?"

Oliver sighed. "Today I really do."

After a while the two-lane highway they'd been driving on widened and became a four-lane freeway. Smith looked askance at Oliver. "You look like a man with a lot on his mind," he said.

"It's been a crazy couple of days," Oliver admitted.

"Woman trouble?"

Oliver laughed. "You could say that. A woman bit me right here," he said, pointing to his neck where Chantal had drawn his blood.

Smith peered at it. "Looks okay to me."

Oliver flipped the passenger visor down and looked in the mirror that was mounted there. His neck was untouched. There wasn't even so much as a bruise. "Huh," he said. Even his shirt was clean; there was no trace of blood anywhere. For a moment he was baffled, then he realized it must have burned off and left his clothes untouched. That was a neat trick.

"You sure you ain't been drinking?"

"No, I'm fine," Oliver said. "You ever have one of those days where…I don't know…it's like you shut your eyes and when you open them again, the world is different?"

"How's that?"

"I mean, it's like the whole world has fundamentally

changed when you weren't looking," Oliver said. "I'm not sure how to explain it."

Smith thought about it. "Like when your kids grow up?"

"No. Like one minute everything is normal, and the next you've got a cat talking to you. And for some reason, that's not even weird. You don't freak out. It makes sense that the cat can talk. It's like the cat could always talk, and you just now noticed."

Smith regarded Oliver nervously. "All right, then," he said.

They drove on in silence. Oliver saw a road sign announcing that they were about to enter Portsmouth. They'd crossed into New Hampshire, then. He hadn't noticed where the state line had been, but today New Hampshire was just as good as Maine. Smith took an off-ramp just outside of the city and pulled into a gas station. "You want to get this one, buddy?" Smith asked, stopping adjacent to a pump.

"Sure," Oliver said. It was the least he could do, he thought. He'd be happy to buy the gas all the way to Boston as long as Smith didn't turn out to be a vampire, or a werewolf, or some kind of alien.

Oliver used a credit card at the pump and then went inside the station to buy snacks and sodas for he and Smith to share. When he came back outside, he was not entirely surprised to find that Smith was gone. He couldn't blame the man. He must have sounded like a complete lunatic before, with the talking cat business and all that.

There was a working pay phone just outside the gas station's front doors. Oliver used it to call 411 and had them connect him to a taxi company. Half an hour later he was in the back of a cab heading into Portsmouth. This time he resolved to keep his mouth shut about anything remotely metaphysical. It wasn't worth the trouble.

Oliver couldn't recall if Portsmouth had been on the itinerary when he'd been on vacation with his parents, but he knew he didn't plan on staying here long. "Is there an airport here?" he asked the cab driver.

"Pease," the man said.

Oliver was taken aback. "Okay, is there an airport here, please?"

"No, no," the driver said. "It's called Pease. Portsmouth International."

"Great." An international airport sounded promising. "Who goes there? American? United?"

"Nothing commercial," the driver said. "It's just general aviation and freight, I think."

Oliver sighed. "Just take me to a hotel, then. I don't care which one. Just something decent."

"The Sheraton is nice," the driver offered.

"The Sheraton, then."

The driver hadn't lied. The Sheraton was perfectly acceptable, if a little smaller in size than Oliver was accustomed to. But he remembered that he was in New England, and the skyscrapers that dotted San Francisco's skyline simply didn't exist here. He inquired about a room at the front desk, only to be told the Honeymoon Suite was the only room available.

"I'll take it," Oliver said, slapping a credit card down on the counter.

"But…" the clerk began. "It's the Honeymoon Suite."

"Do I have to be married to get the room?" he asked.

"No, but it's for newlyweds."

Oliver sighed deeply. "Let me ask you something. Do you think there is a newlywed couple out there, anywhere in the world, that is worried right now because they didn't reserve this particular room? 'Oh, honey, this is the happiest day of my life, but I forgot to reserve the hotel room in Portsmouth!' Seriously?"

The clerk looked less than amused. "No."

"Well, you never know," Oliver said. "Maybe there is. Give me the room, and if those entirely unlikely people do show up here, I'll let them have it. It'll be my gift to them."

Oliver showed the clerk his driver's license and was quickly off to his room, feeling more than a little ashamed of himself. He wasn't usually that sarcastic with strangers. Or at all, he thought. But he'd been through a lot, and he thought maybe he was entitled to a bit of abruptness. Just a bit, mind you. He wouldn't want to make it a habit.

The suite was on the hotel's highest floor, which was to say it was on the third floor. Oliver wasn't sure what all the fuss had been about. The room's door had a plaque bolted to it that read "Honeymoon Suite," but that was the most romantic thing about it. The furnishings inside were entirely what he would have expected. There was one ordinary queen bed, which was definitely not formed in the shape of a heart or covered in red satin sheets. There was a perfectly acceptable television and an armoire against one wall. Maybe they dressed the place up when they had a reservation, Oliver thought.

Flower petals and chocolates on the bed, or something like that. He wasn't sure what hotels usually did.

Oliver checked inside the minibar and helped himself to a four-dollar can of diet soda. He flipped on the television and looked through the channels, none of which interested him. He spent a moment watching CNN to see if there was anything odd in the news, be it lizards or vampires or magical doors appearing out of nowhere. It was entirely ordinary. Democrats and Republicans didn't like each other, and there was trouble in the Middle East. Same as every other day. Oliver was almost disappointed.

He dialed room service and ordered a turkey sandwich with a side of steak fries, which arrived promptly fifteen minutes later. Oliver tore into it with the vigor of a starving man. He hadn't realized until the smell of food hit him how hungry he really was.

Oliver turned the television to one of the local cable channels, which was running a marathon of a detective series. He'd seen the current episode already. Deciding he'd earned it, he went back to the minibar and spent five dollars on a package of M&M's for dessert. He thought about it for a moment, then took two miniature bottles of Scotch as well. He knew the alcohol was absurdly overpriced, but he no longer cared. He downed them one after the other and watched the television detective get one step closer to finding the murderer.

Half an hour later he switched off the television and lay back on the bed. He was tired. When was the last time he'd gone to sleep without the unwanted assistance of drugs? He couldn't remember now, and he didn't care. Oliver sighed deeply and drifted off to sleep.

And for the first time in his life, Oliver dreamed.

Chapter 15

Oliver found himself in a lecture hall, seated in a padded chair equipped with a tablet arm. He looked around, surprised. He'd been here before. He was at his university, Fordham Heights College. This room was in the humanities wing, if he remembered correctly. It had been packed the last time he'd been in here, but now he was the only student in the class.

The room had a pitched floor so as to increase the available seating. At the lowest level stood a podium, with a blackboard just behind it. Behind the podium stood Dr. Thomas, his old astronomy professor.

"Good morning, Mr. Jones," said the professor.

"Good morning, Dr. Thomas," said Oliver politely. This was a dream, wasn't it? His first dream? Weren't you supposed to be able to pinch yourself to see if you were dreaming? Oliver hesitated, then reached down and pinched his own leg. "Ow," he said. That had hurt. Wait, did feeling pain mean that it was a dream or not a dream? He couldn't remember.

"What did you think of the reading?" his professor asked, holding up a thin volume. Oliver leaned forward so he could read the title. The book was *A Brief History of Time*, by Stephen Hawking. Oliver remembered it. It had been assigned as part of his "Great Works" class, which had been mandatory for all freshmen in his school. The assigned readings had included authors such as Shakespeare, Tolstoy, and for some reason, Stephen Hawking.

"I thought it was difficult," Oliver said honestly. He had.

"What struck you the most?"

"Well," Oliver began. It was difficult to say, given how little of it he had understood. "We had been talking about mass-energy equivalence before."

"And what conclusion can we draw?"

"Physics is hard," replied Oliver.

"Dumbass" jeered a new voice. Oliver looked at the desk nearest to him. Jeffrey was sitting on top of it, looking back at him. Now Oliver was positive he was dreaming. He'd have remembered if a talking cat had been in his class. People remembered that kind of thing.

"What conclusion can we draw?" Jeffrey asked.

Oliver looked at his desk. An empty sheet of paper and a pen lay before him. Was he supposed to write something down?

"Matter cannot be created or destroyed," Oliver said.

"And that would be impressive if I were teaching third-grade science," said Dr. Thomas sternly. "However, I am not."

"I'm not sure why you're teaching Stephen Hawking in a

literature class," Oliver pointed out.

"What conclusion can we draw?" Dr. Thomas repeated.

"I remember this question," Oliver said. "I answered it before. I gave you a conclusion."

"What conclusion can we draw?"

"I said that thought was a form of energy, and therefore mass."

"And?"

"That if thought and mass were equivalent, I asked you if thought could somehow be transformed into mass?"

"Very good," said Dr. Thomas.

"No," said Oliver. "It's wrong. You laughed. You made me feel like an idiot."

"Imagine that," said Jeffrey.

"You said it was 'absurd.' That's a quote, by the way. You said if it were true, you would think about Pamela Anderson and Pamela Anderson would appear."

"Who is Pamela Anderson?" asked Jeffrey.

Oliver sighed. "I can't remember the rest of what you said. You drew a bunch of equations on the board and I got a B in your stupid class. A *literature* class, by the way."

"Who is Pamela Anderson?" Jeffrey demanded.

"She was a model a long time ago," Oliver told the cat. "She used to be on a television show about lifeguards. I never actually saw it."

"What did she look like?"

"I don't really remember," Oliver admitted. "Um...tall. Blonde. Kinda pretty, I guess. She was mostly famous for her big brea...she was curvy."

"Oh," Jeffrey said. He looked at the front of the classroom. "Like her?"

Oliver blinked. Dr. Thomas was gone. In his place stood a tall, curvy blonde woman. It definitely was not Pamela Anderson, but he didn't care. She was gorgeous, and she was smiling invitingly at Oliver.

"Wow," Oliver said. "Some dream."

"No fair!" cried Jeffrey. "Make someone for me, too! Maybe a sleek little Siamese. No, *two* sleek little Siamese!"

"You can't make things appear by thinking about them," Oliver scolded the cat.

Jeffrey looked at the smiling blonde woman, then back at Oliver. "Are you sure?" he asked.

Oliver wondered. This was only a dream, after all. In that case, who knew what else he could do?

The blonde woman reached down and rapped her knuckles sharply on the podium. Oliver felt the world starting to slip. What was happening now?

The rapping came a second time, and Oliver opened his eyes. He was back in his room at the Sheraton. Jeffrey and Dr. Thomas were nowhere to be seen, nor was the blonde woman. It had been a dream, of course. Was *that* what dreaming was like? It seemed overrated.

The rapping came a third time. "Who is it?" Oliver asked.

"Room service," called a man's voice from behind the

door.

"They already came," Oliver said, getting off the bed. Then he frowned. That voice had sounded awfully familiar.

Oliver crossed the room to the door and opened it cautiously. Sally and Tyler were standing on the other side. "Don't just open the door like that," Sally scolded him. "You didn't know who we were." But Tyler came forward and swept Oliver up in a bear hug.

"Good to see you," Tyler said. He was wearing a new Hawaiian shirt, Oliver noted. The last one must have been destroyed when...what was the proper word for turning into a bipedal wolf monster?

"Thanks," Oliver said awkwardly. "It's good to see you, too." Oddly enough, Oliver found that he meant it.

"We could have been anyone," Sally continued, pushing her way past them into the room. "Never just open the door."

"But you knocked."

"Oh, god," she sighed. She looked around the room. "Anyone else here?"

Oliver shut the door behind them once Tyler had come inside. "No. How did you guys find me?"

Tyler gave him a guilty look. "I put a tracker on your clothes earlier," he admitted.

"You...you *bugged* me?" Oliver asked.

"For lack of a better word, yeah."

"Oh." Oliver wondered how Tyler had done that without him noticing. Maybe it had happened when he was unconscious.

"That's the last thing we need to worry about," Sally said. She turned to Oliver. "What happened at John Blackwell's house?" she asked.

"A vampire bit me," Oliver said. Then he started to laugh.

Tyler and Sally exchanged a worried glance. "And...how is that funny?" Tyler asked.

Oliver continued laughing. "I just can't believe I said that," he replied. "A vampire bit me. Do you know how ridiculous that sounds?" He sighed deeply. "Fuck my life. Who would believe any of this?"

"Try doing my job someday," Tyler muttered. Sally nodded. Neither of them seemed to find the situation all that humorous, Oliver noted. Or all that unusual.

"What happened after that?" Sally asked.

"It gets weird," Oliver said. "Weirder, I should say."

"Yeah?" Tyler asked.

"I wanted to leave but the door was blocked by...vampires."

"And?" Sally asked expectantly.

"Um..." Oliver wasn't sure how to phrase the next part. "A door magically appeared and I walked through it." He frowned. That had sounded even crazier said out loud than it had in his head.

"Well then," said Sally.

"Yeah," Tyler said. "That's about what Blackwell told us."

"You went back for me?"

"We never had to," Tyler said. "Seven started flipping his shit because your signal hopped from California to the East Coast in the space of about three seconds, and Artemis got the call a minute and a half later. Blackwell told her what happened."

"What did she say?" Oliver asked.

Sally snorted and looked away. "She politely asked whether he knew what the word 'protection' meant," Tyler said.

"Really?"

"She may not have been polite," Tyler said.

"Well, that's what happened," Oliver said.

"So how did you do it?" Sally asked.

"I have no idea. My head was a mess. They drugged me and the blood was...like another drug. I guess I...*teleported*, somehow?"

"Teleportation doesn't exist, as far as I know," Tyler said. "The cyborgs came close to developing it once, but they never got it to work."

"And there aren't any more cyborgs," Oliver said, remembering.

"No, there aren't," Sally smiled.

"It doesn't sound like teleportation, anyway," Tyler said. "It sounds like a portal was opened. That *is* a thing, but damned if I know anyone that can pull it off without some pretty serious tools."

"Is the door still there, in the house?" Oliver asked. "It didn't appear in Maine."

"No, it vanished as soon as you left," Tyler said. "Blackwell said he'd never seen anything like it. He asked if you were a sorcerer."

"People keep saying that," Oliver said. "Well, vampires and my cat say it. Are there really sorcerers out there?"

"I guess so," Tyler shrugged. "I never met one."

"So are you a vampire now?" Sally asked him.

"No," Oliver said. "Well, I don't think so. I've been out in the sun. Doesn't that kill vampires?"

"Not immediately, but you'd have a nasty sunburn," Tyler said. "You look all right. So she just drained you?"

"No," said Oliver. "She made me drink her blood. She wanted to turn me into one of them, but it didn't work."

"I'll be damned," said Tyler. "I've never heard of it just 'not working' before. Not and the victim still being alive, anyway." He looked at Oliver suspiciously. "You have any new cravings? Rare meat? Virgins?"

"No, I…" Oliver blinked in surprise. "*Virgins?*"

"He doesn't know all that much about vampires," Sally said. "Neither do I, really."

"But you know one," Oliver pointed out. "You drove right to his house!"

"You think we hang out there?" Tyler asked. "Hell, no. And when *you* go to somebody's house, do you start asking about their medical history? Or whether they can turn into a bat? Of course you don't. Half the mythology about them is crap, I know that much. At least half."

"Did you have a twin?" Sally asked suddenly.

"No," Oliver said. "Why?"

"Forget it," she said. She looked at Tyler. "So he's immune to vampirism and he makes magic doors."

"And cats that talk," Oliver pointed out.

"And cats that talk," she said. "You got any ideas on this?" she asked Tyler.

"Zilch," said Tyler. "Look, I'll be honest," he said to Oliver. "We're flying by the seat of our pants here. But Artemis is committed to keeping you safe. We should take you out of here."

"Where?" Oliver asked. "Back to the vampires? That didn't work out so well."

"Chantal won't bother you again," Sally said. "Maria took her head off."

"Well, I think she deserved a little..." Oliver paused. "Wait, you don't mean she got yelled at, do you?"

"No," Sally said grimly. "I don't."

"Oh," Oliver said.

"Anyway, Artemis wants you kept mobile," Tyler continued. "At least until she figures out what the lizards are up to."

"Great," Oliver said. "If your little girl can't solve it, you could always call Encyclopedia Brown."

Tyler blinked in surprise. "You getting a little punchy?" Sally asked him.

"Ah, I'm sorry," Oliver said. "It's been a weird couple of

days. What day is it, anyway? I only meant to take a nap but if you got here from California already…"

"It's Friday night," Tyler said.

So he'd been asleep most of the day, Oliver thought. That wasn't what he'd intended to do, but his body had probably needed the rest.

There was a sudden knock at the door. "You expecting someone?" Tyler asked.

"I wasn't expecting *you*," Oliver pointed out. "Who is it?" he called.

"Room service," replied a man's voice.

"I didn't order…" Oliver began, but then he paused. That voice had been familiar, as well.

"Oh, shit," Tyler said. Sally's hands darted into her jacket pockets and came out with her silver pistols.

The knock at the door was repeated. "Open the door, Mr. Jones," said Mr. Teasdale. "I'm not going to hurt you. Besides, you really don't have anywhere to go."

Oliver looked around the room desperately. He was on the top floor and there was no other way out of here. Mr. Teasdale was right. He had nowhere to go.

Chapter 16

"How the hell did he find me?" Oliver asked. Tyler had said he and Sally had found him by following a "tracker" they'd placed on his clothes. Could the assassin have done the same thing? Oliver started to pat himself down before he realized he'd never even noticed the first device. He had little chance of finding a second.

Sally's expression darkened. "You've been using credit cards, haven't you?" she asked.

"Of course," Oliver said. "I had to pay for the room. Oh, and I bought gas this morning."

She sighed. "That's how. The charges left an electronic trail and he followed it right to you."

There was another knock at the door. "Mr. Jones? I'm waiting."

"You want to try that magic door thing again?" Tyler asked. "See if you can get us out of here?"

"I don't know how!" Oliver insisted.

"Tap your heels together three times," Sally sneered. She leveled her pistols at the door and nodded to Tyler. "Open it."

"You're just going to let him in?" Oliver asked. *That* was her plan? Opening the door and letting the assassin come in had to be the worst plan of all time.

"There's no other way out of here," Sally pointed out. "So unless you've got a better idea, let's just get this over with."

Oliver backed away from the door and stood near the window. Tyler drew his own pistol, then unlatched the door and quickly stepped back.

The door swung open slowly. Mr. Teasdale stood there, a small smile on his face. He was carrying his briefcase and still wore the same black suit and red tie Oliver had seen him in yesterday. He wondered if the man ever wore anything else.

The man's skin looked as ill-fitting as it had the day before, but there was no sign that there ever had been so much as a scratch on his head, much less the bullet wound that Oliver had seen yesterday. Oliver wasn't sure what to make of that. In a world where vampires and werewolves were just outside walking around like everyone else, who knew what else could be out in the world? Teasdale could be something he had never even heard of before.

Mr. Teasdale frowned at the sight of Tyler and Sally, along with the small arsenal they had aimed at him. He made a small *tsk* sound with his tongue. "I must say, this does not make me feel very welcome at all."

"Come on in," Tyler said.

"And close the door behind you," Sally continued.

Mr. Teasdale stepped into the room, not seeming to care that two people were standing ready to shoot him inside it. He closed the door behind him and smiled pleasantly at Oliver. "Nice to see you again, Mr. Jones."

"Thanks," said Oliver. "Nice to…" he began automatically, before cutting himself off. He really needed to work on being less polite.

Mr. Teasdale turned to Sally. "It has been a while, Sally Rain."

"So it has," she said.

"I had been meaning to tell you that while certain parties were unhappy with your recent…indiscretion…I myself could not help but admire the artistry of it." He nodded slightly. "True genocide is such a rare thing, and it is something to be savored."

Oliver blinked. Genocide? He must mean the cyborgs everyone kept going on about. What had happened with the cyborgs, anyway?

Sally looked unfazed. "Thank you," she said. She did not lower her pistols.

Tyler stepped in front of Oliver. "You obviously can't kill him with us here to stop you. You lose this round. Get in the bathroom, shut the door, and don't come out until we're gone."

Mr. Teasdale turned and regarded him coldly. "Mr. Jacobsen. You shot me," he scolded the other man.

"I'll do it again," Tyler said.

"And it still won't kill me," Teasdale said. He sighed and

made a conciliatory gesture with his hand. "I will forgive you for yesterday. We were both doing as our respective professions dictate, and therefore it would not be appropriate for me to perceive it as a personal insult." His eyes were cold. "However, I will not forgive you a second time."

Oliver frowned. "But you're still both doing what your respective professions dictate," he pointed out.

"I am not," the assassin said. "The Kalatari violated the terms of our contract."

"They did?" Tyler asked.

Sally suddenly gasped. "Of course. They told you it was a mistake, then they killed that other guy and went after Oliver themselves." The edge of her mouth twitched up into a crooked smile. "They lied to you."

"They *lied*," Mr. Teasdale hissed. He looked genuinely angry. "Lying is not permitted once a contract has been established."

Tyler lowered his pistol. Sally did not lower either of hers. "So why are you here?" she asked.

Teasdale raised his briefcase. "I have brought an offering for Mr. Jones," he said.

"I have a briefcase already," Oliver said.

Teasdale sighed and gestured at the bed. "May I?"

Oliver nodded. Teasdale crossed the room and lay the briefcase down flat. He clicked the latches and was starting to open the case when Sally stopped him, gesturing with her pistols. "Slowly."

"As you will, Ms. Rain." Teasdale opened the case slowly.

He reached inside and for an instant Oliver thought he was going to come out with a weapon, but instead he held up a small spherical object wrapped in white cloth. "For you, Mr. Jones. Payment for a broken contract."

Oliver shook his head. "That doesn't make sense. We never had a contract."

"*We* were not required to establish one," Teasdale said. "When the Kalatari broke my contract, they became the target of that contract. Rules are rules, Mr. Jones."

"Oh my god," Tyler said, looking at the wrapped object Teasdale held in sudden horror.

"What is that?" Oliver asked, nodding at the sphere.

Teasdale held the object up in one hand, the other poised above it as if to unwrap a birthday present. "If I may?" he asked, glancing at Sally. She nodded. Oliver watched them with a sense of foreboding. What did he mean, the Kalatari had become the target of his contract? Exactly what rules did this man play by?

Teasdale began unwrapping Oliver's "offering," revealing a small fleshy red thing the size of a fist. It looked oddly familiar to Oliver, but he was sure he hadn't seen anything exactly like it before.

Tyler turned away, looking queasy. Sally leaned forward. "Oh, that is nice," she said, her eyes widening.

"What is it?" Oliver asked, not understanding.

"It's a heart," Tyler groaned.

"What?"

"A heart," Mr. Teasdale confirmed. "Specifically, it is the

heart of Sathis Rin, formerly chief minister to the Kalatari matriarch." He noted Oliver's confused expression. "The man who ordered your death," Teasdale explained.

Oliver felt his stomach flip-flop. "That's a heart?"

"That has been established."

"A lizard heart?"

"I am not a biologist, but as I know that by 'lizard' you mean the Kalatari race, yes. A lizard heart."

Oliver wasn't sure what to say. "It's not bloody." He was instantly frustrated with himself. Was that really the best remark he could come up with?

Mr. Teasdale looked offended. "Of course it isn't bloody, Mr. Jones. I cleaned it for you. We are not barbarians." He extended his hand, offering the heart to Oliver.

"Um...on the table is fine," Oliver said quickly.

Teasdale sighed and placed the heart delicately on the desk. "I have no personal knowledge of this," he mused, "but I have been told that they are quite lovely stewed with star anise and cinnamon."

Oliver blinked in surprise. "You think I'm going to eat it?" he asked.

"I did not think you were going to mount it on your wall," Teasdale replied. "Although I suppose there is no reason you could not," he continued thoughtfully.

"Okay, then," Oliver said.

Teasdale waited expectantly. Oliver wondered if he wanted a tip. "Am I supposed to pay you?" he asked finally. Was that part of the contract as well? Who was Teasdale going to kill if he didn't have enough money? What was the going price on lizard hearts these days?

Mr. Teasdale sighed as if he were dealing with a stupid child. "Typically, Mr. Jones, one says 'thank you' when one has just been presented with a heart."

"Oh. Okay. Well, thank you."

"You are welcome." Teasdale snapped his briefcase shut. "Well then, I will be off. Good bye, Mr. Jones, Ms. Rain." He nodded at each of them in turn. Then he turned to Tyler. "Mr. Jacobsen, if you ever shoot me again I will cut your face off and wear it as a mask to frighten children on Halloween. Are we clear?"

Tyler swallowed hard. "Clear," he said, fingering his pistol.

"Farewell then," Teasdale said, moving toward the door.

"Wait!" Oliver called after him. Teasdale stopped and looked back at Oliver curiously. "Did he tell you why?" Oliver asked. "Why they want me dead? I mean, before you killed him."

"Oh," Teasdale said. He shrugged. "He claimed that the Matriarch had a prophetic vision. She called you the 'destroyer of worlds' and foresaw that you would murder their entire race."

Oliver tried not to look as startled as he felt. "I see."

"I wouldn't worry about it, Mr. Jones," Teasdale reassured him. "The Matriarch is known to indulge in a variety of hallucinogens. Her prophecies never come to anything."

Oliver took that as good news. "So it's a mistake, then?" he asked tentatively. "They're not going to kill me?"

"Oh my no, Mr. Jones," Teasdale replied. "I meant I am sure you are not going to exterminate them. But they will certainly kill you." With that, Teasdale nodded politely and went through the door, disappearing shortly down the hall.

Tyler looked at Sally. "That went better than I expected."

She shrugged. "I kind of wanted to shoot him. Just to see what would happen."

"I shot him yesterday. It didn't do much."

"Maybe you didn't shoot him *enough*," Sally suggested.

"What exactly *is* he?" Oliver asked. "Do either of you know?"

"I have no idea," said Tyler. "Something old and powerful, that's for certain."

"Artemis might know," Sally said. "If not, I don't know who you'd ask."

"And I still can't believe his name is Hilary Teasdale," Oliver continued. "He sounds like the villain in a Three Stooges movie."

"Oh yeah?" asked Tyler. "I always saw him with the Marx Brothers."

"Who are the Marx Brothers?" asked Sally.

Tyler and Oliver both turned to stare at her. "Really?" asked Tyler.

Sally scowled at them. "Forget it."

"How could you possibly not know..." Oliver began.

"Forget it," Sally warned.

"Anyway, we can't stay here," Tyler said. "If he was able to find you here, whoever else the Kalatari have after you won't be far behind."

"So back to running," Oliver sighed. "You brought a car, I suppose?"

"Better than that," Tyler said. "We brought a plane."

Chapter 17

Five minutes later they were on the sidewalk trying to hail a taxi. They were on a major street, or at least what passed for a major street in Portsmouth, but they hadn't seen a single cab go by yet. Sally looked annoyed. "It's like they've never heard of a taxi line here," she said.

"It's Portsmouth," Oliver told her. "I doubt there's a taxi line anywhere in the city." It was hard to imagine any place here needing one.

"It's worse than San Francisco," she complained.

"Nothing is worse than getting a taxi in San Francisco," Tyler said. Oliver nodded. He'd heard people use the difficulty of getting a cab in San Francisco as an argument for buying a car. He'd never believed things were that bad until he'd been late for work one morning and decided to call a cab instead of taking the train. After waiting an hour for it to arrive he'd called to cancel it, and then called in sick to work.

Sally went into the hotel and spoke to the front desk clerk.

"They're calling one," she said when she returned. "Next time we get a rental."

"They didn't have a rental place at Pease," Tyler protested.

"Then we buy a damn car," Sally said.

The taxi came at last, a sedan that was far too small to seat the three of them in the rear. Sally sat next to the driver and they started toward the airport.

"Werewolf?" Oliver asked suddenly.

Startled, Tyler looked out the window. "Where?"

"No," Oliver said. "Do you think Mr. Teasdale is a werewolf?"

"Oh," Tyler said. "You scared me for a minute."

"Sorry."

"No, he's not."

That made sense, Oliver thought. "You'd be able to smell it if he was?"

Tyler frowned. "I'm not sure. Maybe. It's never really come up."

"Are there a lot of werewolves?" Oliver asked.

Oliver noted the cab driver's confused expression in the rear view mirror. He'd gotten far too casual in talking about these things openly, he realized. He'd have to be more careful about that.

Sally had noticed the driver's look as well. "Those two are in town for a convention," she said to the driver. "For...people who like to dress up in animal costumes. What that's called."

"Furries?" asked Tyler.

"Yeah," Sally said.

"We're not furries!" Tyler protested.

"Yeah, you are," Sally said. "Especially him," she said to the driver, nodding at Tyler. "He's the biggest furry I've ever seen. He *loves* it."

"Oh," the driver said, nodding a bit uneasily. "Well, different strokes and all."

"That's right," said Sally, looking out the window. "Hey, guys, why don't we talk about something else for a while? Like, *anything* else?"

Oliver had many more questions but decided they could wait until they were in private. He found that in a way he was becoming accustomed to getting strange answers to simple questions. He wasn't sure there was anything more that could happen that would truly surprise him.

That wasn't a good thing, was it? He frowned. Earlier he had thought perhaps he'd suffered some kind of brain injury and was imagining all of these things. He no longer felt that way, but then how could he explain his newfound calmness? Shock? Was it possible that he was in shock?

Tyler's cell phone chirped. He answered it and listened for a moment. "Artemis," he said, ending the call. "She wants us in the air."

"We're about to be," Sally said. "Where are we going?"

"Nowhere. Just up."

"Just up?" asked Oliver. "What does that mean?"

"The Kalatari can't fly," Tyler explained. "Up is about the safest place we can be. She'll let us know when and where to land."

Oliver thought about it. He had to admit, it made sense. The Kalatari weren't going to be able to find him if he was 40,000 feet up in the air.

"That's a funny name," the cab driver mused.

"Kalatari?" Tyler asked. Sally gave him a dark look. "Oh, that's just the name of my..." he struggled to find a word. "Um...furry friend..."

"No," the driver said. "Artemis."

"Oh," Tyler said. "Yeah, I guess. It's an old Greek name."

"So she's Greek?" Oliver asked.

"For god's sake," Sally sighed. "She's not Greek. Does she look Greek to you?"

Oliver didn't think Greeks were typically pale-skinned and blond, but he also wasn't sure he actually knew any Greek people. "No," he said. "But you never know. People don't expect Italians to be blond, but in Northern Italy it's pretty common." Oliver had never been to Italy. He'd discovered this by watching the Travel Channel.

Tyler was considering it, though. "I don't know," he said. "Things change over time. We don't actually know what the Greeks looked like when..." he stopped abruptly, glancing at the driver. "Forget it."

"Why don't one of you just ask her?" Oliver asked. Sally snorted, and Tyler just stared at him. "What?" Oliver asked. "Why was that a crazy question?"

Neither of them answered. "It's a pretty name," the cab driver mused. "Wouldn't name my own kid that, but it's kind of nice."

It didn't take long to reach the city limits of Portsmouth and they were quickly out on the freeway. Oliver wondered when he would get to the East Coast again. This had been quite an unexpected trip; he'd like to come back and spend some proper time out here.

Or perhaps he was just being nostalgic, he thought. He'd been here with his family, and he hadn't seen any of them in a while. He'd have to do something about that, provided he lived through the next few days.

The rest of the trip passed in silence until they reached Pease, which was a small general aviation airport used by tiny propeller-driven planes and small jets. Oliver did spot a large FedEx terminal with larger planes and recalled hearing somewhere that FedEx had the second largest fleet of airplanes in the world. He wondered if that were really true, or where he'd heard it. Perhaps on the Travel Channel.

Oliver sighed. Had he learned everything he knew from late-night television? If he did live through this, he was definitely going to change his life. Forget taking a cooking class; he'd take ten classes. Maybe he'd get another degree and try to find a job he actually liked. The dull life he'd been living for so long just wouldn't work for him anymore.

Tyler directed the taxi driver to a small Learjet parked near a tiny hangar. Oliver wondered what their group's operating budget was like. This couldn't have been cheap. "Is this your plane?" he asked.

"It's a charter," Sally said. "We have our own plane, but it's in the shop."

"Oh. Maintenance?"

"No," Tyler shook his head, looking at Sally. "Someone crashed it."

"Shut up," Sally grumbled.

Tyler gave the driver his fare and a very excessive tip. He stretched luxuriously after the cab had driven off. "It's a clear night," he said, looking up at the sky. "You guys ready to check out the stars?"

"Is it a full moon?" Oliver asked. "We could be in some trouble if you wolf out on us up there."

Sally laughed as Tyler scowled. "That's not funny," he said.

"You're all right, Oliver," Sally admitted. "I'm glad I didn't shoot you earlier."

"Thanks," Oliver said. "I guess."

Tyler looked at Oliver appraisingly. "It's funny how well you're taking this, Oliver," Tyler said.

"What?"

"All of this," Tyler said. "Every crazy thing that has happened to you in the last two days. If you think about it, your whole world has been torn apart."

"True," Sally said.

"It's not that I expected you to go catatonic," Tyler continued, "but I don't mind telling you, when it was *my* life being turned upside down, I didn't do so well."

"Yeah, but you were turning into a dog," Sally grinned. "That would get to anybody."

Tyler looked at her for a long moment. "You know something?" he asked, and Oliver could hear emotion in his voice. "It's really nice to see you smile again."

Sally opened her mouth to say something, but shut it again abruptly. She looked away and for the briefest of moments Oliver thought he saw her bottom lip tremble, but then it was gone. "We should go," she said.

"Yeah," Tyler nodded.

There was a removable metal staircase laid out with steps leading up to the jet's open door. Oliver stepped up first. He had to admit he liked the idea of just flying around for a while. Unless the Kalatari had access to fighter planes or missiles, there was probably no safer place he could be.

A sharply dressed flight attendant smiled at him as he stepped into the cabin. "Good evening, Mr. Jones," he said. "Right down there, please." He motioned to the row of seats behind him. The jet had seating capacity for perhaps ten people, with one seat on each side of a narrow aisle. There was nobody else visible in the plane. Oliver assumed that the pilots must already be in the cockpit. Not a bad setup, he thought. They had brought along a flight attendant? He wondered if they had snacks as well. Oliver had missed out on dinner. Skipping mealtimes seemed to be becoming a habit.

"Hey, who the hell are you?" he heard Tyler asking behind him. Oliver turned around and saw that the flight attendant was now brandishing two pistols. One was pointed out the door at where Tyler was presumably standing on the stairs, and the other was pointed directly at Oliver himself. "Nobody move," the flight attendant said.

The cockpit door swung open and a heavyset man in jeans

emerged holding a shotgun. He did not look like a pilot, Oliver observed. The man pointed his weapon out the door. "Get back," he shouted at Tyler. "Back now!"

There was some commotion on the stairs that Oliver couldn't see. The heavyset man lowered his weapon and seized the door handle. He pulled the door shut with a loud grunt. Oliver was trapped inside with them now. His friends wouldn't be able to do anything to help him.

"Well done," said a new voice from just behind Oliver. Oliver turned and was nearly struck mute by what he saw. A man, if that was the right word, stood there, having just emerged from the rear lavatory. He'd probably been hiding back there, Oliver realized. The man was roughly Oliver's height, and had roughly the same proportions. Two arms. Two legs. One head. But the head was hairless, with leathery, dark green skin covered by small, tightly overlapping scales. He had yellow eyes with black, vertical pupils. The man had no nose, but a rounded muzzle in its place with two vertical slits where nostrils might have been. As he smiled Oliver could see that his mouth was full of small, jagged teeth.

"Take off," the lizard man nodded to the man with the shotgun. Oliver watched as the heavyset man disappeared back into the cockpit, shutting the door behind him.

"Oliver Jones," the lizard man said, a forked tongue darting out from between his teeth. "My mistress is eager to meet you."

The sight of the forked tongue was too much for Oliver. He didn't want to. He tried to stop it. But despite himself, he began to laugh.

Chapter 18

Oliver realized two things almost immediately. The first was that he was laughing at what was essentially a monster bent on murdering him. That couldn't be especially wise. The second was that he didn't recognize his own laugh anymore. The sound coming out of his mouth was high-pitched and had an element of hysteria in it that he'd never heard before. This was what laughter in an asylum must sound like, he thought. It was the laughter of a madman.

"Oh my god," Oliver managed to say. He was nearly out of breath and had leaned forward to rest his hands on his knees.

The lizard man tilted his head curiously. "What is it?"

"Captain Kirk called," Oliver said. "He wants his diamonds back." Then he was laughing again.

The Kalatari's expression darkened. He looked accusingly at the flight attendant. "What is this?" he demanded. "Why is he laughing?"

The other man shrugged. "Shock?" he suggested. Oliver

heard the jet's engines beginning to spin up and the plane lurched forward. He nearly had himself under control when something else caught his eye and he began to laugh again.

"Look at you," he said, pointing down. "You're wearing shoes!" Oliver turned to the flight attendant. "Look at his little shoes!" he said.

The Kalatari looked down at his own feet in confusion. "They're Ferragamo," he said.

"Is there a section at Macy's for lizards?"

"He's addled," the Kalatari said with a disgusted expression. "*This* is the Destroyer?"

"Perhaps the Matriarch was wrong," said the flight attendant.

The lizard man's hand disappeared into his jacket and emerged an instant later in a flicking motion. Oliver gasped. A short knife was now embedded firmly in the flight attendant's throat. The other man made a strangled sound as blood spurted from his wound, and then he collapsed to the floor.

"The Matriarch is never wrong," the Kalatari told Oliver, who found he had suddenly recovered from his unwelcome fit of laughter.

Oliver hadn't noticed the jet's rapidly increasing acceleration, and he stumbled a step forward as they lifted off. He braced himself on one of the seats. "Careful," the lizard man said. "Sit down."

Oliver sat. "Put this on," the lizard man said, handing him a zip tie. "Around your wrists. Fasten it tightly."

Oliver looked around the jet's interior. "Where would I

really run to?" he asked the Kalatari. "We're in the air."

"My orders are to bring you in alive. I don't want you panicking and trying to fight me. You might get hurt by accident."

Oliver looped the zip tie around his wrists and pulled it shut with his teeth. "If I haven't panicked yet, I don't think I'm going to start now," he noted.

The lizard man tugged at Oliver's wrists to make sure he was bound securely. "You never know," he said. Then went up the aisle to where the flight attendant had fallen. He knelt down and pulled at his knife until it came free. The Kalatari sniffed the other man's blood on the blade the way some people sniffed at wine, then licked the blood off of it. Oliver shuddered. That *was* kind of disgusting, but hardly enough to make him panic after what he'd seen in the past two days.

Then the lizard man raised the knife and drove it deep into the other man's abdomen. Oliver winced at the sight. "I think you got him," he said to the Kalatari.

The lizard man was making a sawing motion with the knife, opening a long wound. "He's still warm."

"So?"

The lizard man dug his claws savagely into the wound and rooted around for a moment, emerging with the flight attendant's liver. "Some things should be eaten warm," he said.

Oliver suppressed the urge to throw up as the lizard took a bite out of the liver and chewed it. "An alcoholic," the lizard said thoughtfully. "Makes the liver a bit of an acquired taste, but I don't mind." He rose and took the seat across the aisle from Oliver, still munching on the liver. "Feel like panicking yet?" he asked.

"I'm okay," Oliver lied.

The lizard man shrugged. "If you say so."

The plane had leveled off. "How did you find me?" Oliver asked. "The credit cards? Was that it?"

"No," the lizard man said thoughtfully. "Although that would have worked as well. We simply followed your friends back there. When they got on this plane, we weren't far behind. And then they were nice enough to go pick you up for us, so we decided we'd just wait here for them."

"Oh." Oliver thought about it for a moment. "That sounds incredibly easy, actually."

"It was."

"So where are we going?" Oliver asked.

"San Francisco," the Kalatari said. "I will deliver you to my Matriarch at our temple there, and she will deal with you."

"Deal with?" Oliver asked.

"Kill and eat, I expect."

That sounded less than ideal, Oliver thought. But as much as he hadn't wanted to be captured, maybe he could bring something good out of this moment. He finally had a chance to explain the situation to the people who had actually been pursuing him. "Look," he began. "This has all been some kind of mistake. I had never heard of you people until a few days ago. I would never even have imagined you existed. I can't possibly be this 'Destroyer' of yours. I'm just someone who works in an office and eats microwave dinners."

"Really?" the lizard man asked. He shrugged. "Okay, I'll just let you go."

"You will?"

"Of course not. By Vashka, you really are addled."

"I'm not addled." Oliver shrugged. "Or maybe I am. I'm not convinced this isn't all some kind of delusion. Maybe I was hit by a car crossing the street and I have a brain injury."

"That I could believe," the Kalatari said.

"If I could talk to your matriarch, I'm sure I could clear all this up."

"Perhaps you could," the lizard man said. "I admit it is hard to see you as the destroyer of my race. You seem too inept to tie your own shoelaces."

"So you think she'll let me go?"

The lizard man shook his head. "You will have the opportunity to speak. The Matriarch will expect you to beg. You might convince her you are not the person she is seeking."

"But that would mean she was wro…" Oliver stopped, not wanting to take a knife in the throat.

"The mistake would have been mine," the Kalatari explained, "in bringing her the wrong person. In which case I would die for my error, and you would die because my people will be needing a snack."

"Oh," said Oliver. Maybe no good was going to come out of his capture after all.

The cockpit door opened and the heavyset man emerged,

starting violently at the sight of the eviscerated flight attendant. He looked at Oliver accusingly, but the Kalatari held up the half-eaten liver for him to see. The man looked as if he wanted to say something, but merely bowed his head.

"What is it?" the lizard man asked.

"Chief Minister, we will land in five and a half hours."

"Thank you. That will be all."

The other man glanced at Oliver again, then went back into the cockpit. Oliver heard the door latch behind him.

What had he said? "You're Chief Minister?" Oliver asked.

"Oh," the lizard man said. "I had meant to introduce myself earlier, but you were being an idiot. I am Orris Rin, Chief Minister to the Matriarch of the Kalatari. Nice to meet you." He took another bite of the liver.

"Any relation to Sathis Rin?" Oliver asked, remembering the heart Mr. Teasdale had presented him with earlier.

"My hatch-brother. Chief Minister until just recently." The lizard's brow arched curiously. "You knew him?"

"No, not really," Oliver said. Sally had taken Sathis Rin's heart along with her, thinking Artemis might have some use for it. He didn't see the need to share that fact with his captor.

The Kalatari finished eating the flight attendant's liver and belched softly, covering his mouth. "Excuse me," he said. He glanced curiously at Oliver. "Why aren't you afraid?"

"Pardon?"

"Why aren't you afraid? You just saw me eat a human liver. You just saw *me*, for that matter. And I am about to deliver you to my mistress, who will certainly kill you. Why don't you cry? Why don't you beg? I thought perhaps you were too stupid to understand your situation, like one of your docile cows walking into the slaughterhouse, but that clearly isn't the case."

Tyler had asked something similar earlier, Oliver remembered. He still wasn't sure of the answer. Oliver shrugged. "I was at first, when this started," he said. "I think." *Had* he been frightened? He wasn't so sure now. He had *reacted*, of course, but now he couldn't remember if he had felt real fear.

"And now?"

"Now it just seems normal," Oliver said. "It's almost like...like I expected all of this."

The Kalatari considered that. "Interesting," he said. "You must watch a lot of television."

"Too much, I guess."

"It was funny, by the way. Earlier."

"What?"

"The Gorn reference. Kirk wants his diamonds back. Funny. Not hilarious, but funny."

"Oh. You didn't think it was mean?"

"Not really. The Gorn would have torn Kirk apart, of course, but it was only a television show."

"Yeah."

"Making fun of my shoes was mean."

"Oh. Well, sorry about that."

"Forget it. I am going to be eating you later, after all." The lizard man shrugged. "You should get some rest, Mr. Jones. We will be landing before you know it."

"Yeah," Oliver said. He sighed. And then this would all be over. He would be dead in a few short hours.

But he still wasn't afraid, he noticed.

Why wasn't he afraid?

Chapter 19

Oliver woke up as the jet began its descent. He was more than a little surprised that he had somehow dozed off, given the precarious circumstances he had found himself in. Events of the past few days must have taken a toll on him, he thought. He had been drugged into unconsciousness twice within the span of a few hours. That had to have been rough on his system. Even now he felt nauseous again, and for a moment he could hear the sound of rushing water in his ears. What was causing that sound? Every time he heard it something bizarre seemed to happen.

He looked around. Nothing bizarre was happening at the moment, aside from the fact that he had been kidnapped by a talking lizard man and was being flown to his almost certain death. Aside from *that*, everything was normal. It was interesting how quickly one's perspective on normalcy could change, he thought.

Orris Rin was still seated next to him, but now he was munching on what looked to Oliver like the remains of a kidney. "We'll be landing soon," the lizard man said.

Oliver peered out of the window. He could make out a city through the clouds below, but it wasn't one he recognized. "That isn't San Francisco."

"Change of plans," the lizard man said. "Your friends beat us to San Francisco."

That was impossible, Oliver thought. How could they have possibly found another plane that quickly? And then they'd managed to not only catch up to them, but pass them in the air and land first? He frowned. Tyler had said they had connections everywhere, but such speeds would have required military cooperation. Had Tyler and Sally gotten their hands on an Air Force jet?

"Why are you so important to them?" the Kalatari asked.

"I don't know," Oliver said truthfully. "I think Artemis likes me because…well, because I'm a curiosity to her. She doesn't know what to make of me, so she wants to keep me alive until she figures it out." That sounded about right. He'd only met the odd little girl once. She certainly wasn't helping him out of some kind of affection.

"That makes you either very lucky, or very unlucky," the lizard man noted.

"Story of my life," Oliver said.

The plane banked sharply. Orris Rin frowned. "Wait here." He went into the cockpit and Oliver could hear raised voices. Then the lizard man returned to his seat, his expression dark. That could only have been bad news, Oliver knew.

"What happened?" Oliver asked.

"Shut up," the lizard man said. He leaned over and tugged at the zip tie still fastened around Oliver's wrists, but found it secure.

"I haven't gone anywhere," Oliver said. "Nowhere to go. What's going on?"

The Kalatari stared sullenly out the window. "Sally Rain attacked our temple."

"Oh?" Had Tyler been with her? What was going on? "Is she all right?" Oliver asked. The lizard man turned to glare at him. "Sorry," Oliver said. "I mean, are your people all right?"

"They are not," Orris Rin said. "She killed a dozen of my brothers and burned our temple to the ground."

"Wow." Oliver didn't know the woman very well, but he had to admit that sounded like something she would do.

"She escaped, since you seem to care." The lizard man leaned in close to Oliver. "Don't imagine that you are going to be rescued, Mr. Jones. I swear to you, if I can't deliver you safely to the Matriarch, I will kill you myself."

Oliver swallowed hard. "Okay."

The lizard sighed and looked out the window again. "I knew going after you was a mistake. I knew it! But the Matriarch..." he trailed off. "The Matriarch is never wrong." Oliver could tell from the Kalatari's expression, though, that he didn't really believe what he was saying at all.

"So where are we landing?"

"Oakland," the lizard said. "Provided that..." he stopped suddenly as the jet's engines whined and the plane began banking again. "What on earth?"

The Kalatari's cell phone buzzed. He answered and listened for a moment. "Understood," he said, hanging up. He looked at Oliver suspiciously. "Are you signaling them somehow?"

"No," Oliver said. "I don't have a phone."

Orris Rin frowned. "Some kind of telepathy?"

Oliver nearly laughed. "No. Why are you..." but he suddenly remembered that Tyler had put a tracking device somewhere on his clothes. Did things like that work when you were airborne? He couldn't think of a reason they wouldn't. They must know exactly where he was.

"They hit our landing site," Orris Rin explained. "We're going to have to think of something else." He went back into the cockpit and shut the door behind him.

Oliver looked out the plane's window. They were much closer to the ground now and getting even closer. The pilot was still taking them down, then. But if they couldn't land in Oakland, where were they going to set down? He knew there had to be other airports in the area, but as long as the tracking device was transmitting, no place would be safe for the Kalatari for very long. Tyler could easily extrapolate their destination just by checking Oliver's trajectory while he was still in the air. There were only so many runways in the Bay Area to choose from.

The plane banked again and Oliver noted that they were descending more quickly now than FAA regulations probably allowed for. He looked at the freeways below, trying to determine their location. There was very little traffic at this hour. Was that I-880 or I-580 below him? They must be heading toward Richmond. How long would it take his new friends to work that out and get there?

Orris Rin emerged from the cockpit and walked back to Oliver's seat. He reached for Oliver's waist, making Oliver jump in surprise, but the lizard man only fastened his seat belt tightly around him. "We're landing," he said.

"Oh." Oliver watched as Orris Rin took his own seat and fastened his belt. "Richmond?"

"In a way," the lizard man said.

Oliver looked down. The freeway was much closer now but there were no runway lights anywhere in sight. Suddenly he knew what Rin had meant. They were going to land in Richmond, but they weren't going to any airport.

"This is insane!" Oliver protested. "You can't land on the freeway!"

"Why not?" the lizard man asked. "Your friends won't be expecting it."

Oliver looked out the window again. The plane would be down in a matter of minutes. They were going to land going in the direction of traffic, he noted. A few cars coming in the other direction had pulled off to the side of the road, no doubt assuming that they were watching a crash landing. Surely somebody was calling 911.

"You may want to hold on," Orris Rin said. Oliver just glared at him.

The plane swerved and Oliver looked out the window to see them passing directly over a trailer truck, close enough that if the door had been open Oliver probably could have jumped onto its top. They'd be on the ground in seconds now. He shut his eyes tightly and waited. Either he was about to hear the screeching of tires, or the sound of metal being torn apart.

There was a thud as the plane's tires hit the pavement and then he heard the familiar whine of airplane braking, which he suddenly felt was the most reassuring sound in the world. Now they just needed enough clear space on the road to slow down safely, but in a plane this size that shouldn't be very much. Nor was it. The plane slid forward a short distance and quickly jerked to a stop. Orris Rin rose from his seat and bent to unfasten Oliver's belt. "Stand up," he said to Oliver. "Quickly."

The cockpit door opened and the heavyset man emerged, again holding his shotgun. He unlocked the lever that secured the door shut and opened it.

"Let's go," said Orris Rin, dragging Oliver to his feet. He pushed Oliver ahead of him up the hallway.

The heavyset man looked down at the street below. "It's a little far," he said to Orris Rin. "We left the stairs back there."

"It doesn't matter. Just jump."

The other man nodded. "What about the body?" he asked, looking at the eviscerated flight attendant.

"Leave him," Orris Rin said. "Go."

The heavyset man turned and jumped out of the airplane. Oliver looked through the door and estimated the drop was only about six feet. It was six feet he didn't want to try and jump with his hands bound, though. "Can you undo this?" he asked Orris Rin, holding up his hands.

"No," said the lizard man, roughly pushing him out the door.

Oliver hadn't been prepared and he hit the ground awkwardly, his leg twisting under him. Unable to brace himself, his body fell sideways and he struck the side of his head on the asphalt. He saw stars and for a moment was sure he would lose consciousness. That wouldn't have been so bad, he thought. He could go to sleep now.

He watched, as if in a trance, as Orris Rin landed on the ground next to him. The lizard man rose and jerked Oliver to his feet.

Oliver felt the world spin. He shut his eyes as Orris Rin pushed him forward. Where were they going? He opened his eyes but found that they wouldn't focus. They were heading toward a car, he thought. He blinked. Yes, a car had parked behind the plane. Another lizard man and a human female were waiting there. They must have coordinated this rendezvous once they knew they couldn't use an airport, Oliver realized. In a moment they'd be on the move and he had no idea how long it would take Tyler to realize that they weren't heading for an airport anymore.

The new lizard man stepped forward and punched Oliver savagely in the face. Oliver's vision went black and his head slumped. "Enough!" he heard Orris Rin shout.

"He burned our temple!" the lizard man shouted.

"*He* didn't burn anything," Orris Rin replied. "Besides, the Matriarch wants him alive."

Oliver opened his eyes. He found they wouldn't focus again. He tried to remember what the symptoms of a concussion were. Did you have to lose consciousness for it to count? He felt his head lolling backwards and he could see the moon above him. *Pretty moon*, he thought.

"Cover his eyes," Orris Rin commanded.

"Why?" Oliver asked. His own voice sounded to him as if it were coming from miles away.

"I'm not convinced you aren't signaling your friends somehow," the lizard man said. "Best if you can't see where we're going." He looked at the heavyset man. "You. Torch the plane."

"I don't have a blindfold," said the other Kalatari. He looked at the woman. "Do you have a blindfold?"

"No."

Orris Rin sighed. "Check the trunk for something." The woman went to the back of the car and Oliver heard the trunk opening.

Oliver looked at Orris Rin, his eyes focusing and then unfocusing again. "You guys are the second worst kidnappers ever," he said woozily.

"What's wrong with him?" the other Kalatari asked. "Is he drunk?"

"You bashed him in the head," Orris Rin said. "He wasn't all that bright to begin with."

The woman returned. "I've got a hat," she said, holding up a San Francisco 49'ers cap.

"You're not the *worst* kidnappers ever," Oliver continued. "Do you want to know who that was?"

"What are we going to do with a hat?" Orris Rin asked. "Never mind. Get him into the car. We need to be out of here before the police or his friends show up."

Oliver was shoved into the car and quickly found himself sandwiched between Orris Rin and the other Kalatari. He put his head back on the seat's headrest and closed his eyes. There was definitely something wrong with him, he thought. He desperately wanted to go to sleep. Everything would be better then.

The heavyset man got behind the wheel of the car with the woman in the passenger seat next to him. They pulled away from the plane, which Oliver dreamily noted was now on fire. "Do you want the hat?" the woman asked. "You could pull it down really far."

"Oh, fine," said Orris Rin. He put the cap on Oliver's head and pulled the brim down over his eyes. Oliver found that he could see only slightly less than he had been able to before. It didn't matter much, as his eyes still weren't focusing.

"Where are we going?" the heavyset man asked.

Orris Rin took out his cell phone and made a call, asking the same question. He listened for a moment, then handed his phone over the seat to the heavyset man, who took it and put it to his ear.

"Got it," the heavyset man said, handing the phone back. "I know the place. I've been there once before."

"Good," said Orris Rin. "Mind the speed limits. We can't afford to be pulled over."

"D.W.L.," Oliver said.

"What?" the Kalatari asked.

"Driving While Lizard," Oliver said, then laughed softly. He shut his eyes, but the world still wouldn't stop spinning. He wondered if it ever would.

Suddenly the heavyset man said, "We're here."

Oliver opened his eyes. Already? They couldn't have gone more than a mile or two. But it was morning now, he saw. The sun was just beginning to peek over the horizon.

He was still in the back seat of the car with the two Kalatari. But the car had stopped and they were in a residential neighborhood, far from the freeway they'd been on the last time he'd had his eyes open.

Had he been unconscious? How much time had passed?

Oliver groaned. His head felt like he'd been hit with a frying pan. "We're where?"

"End of the road, Mr. Jones," Orris Rin said. "Prepare yourself. The Matriarch is waiting for you."

Chapter 20

Orris Rin and the other Kalatari dragged Oliver, still woozy from repeated blows to the head, out of the sedan and onto the sidewalk. They were in front of a small, abandoned church. Its windows had been boarded up and it was in terrible need of a paint job. Oliver could see the remnants of yellow police tape strewn around the church's dirty lawn. It was impossible to tell how long the church had been deserted, but Oliver would have guessed a decade or more.

The two Kalatari were now wearing trench coats and had fedoras pulled down low over their eyes. They looked ridiculous, Oliver thought, but he had to admit that from a distance, nobody would have any idea that they were anything other than ordinary men with seriously questionable fashion sense.

He had obviously been unconscious for a while if the lizard men had found the time to stop and change clothes. He didn't remember that happening at all.

"Where are we?" Oliver asked, looking around. He didn't

recognize the neighborhood and couldn't see any landmarks that would help him get an idea of his location.

"Bakersfield," Orris Rin said.

"Oh." Oliver had never been to Bakersfield and knew little about the city, other than that it was several hours drive south of San Francisco. It was only an hour or two from Los Angeles, if he remembered correctly. They'd had quite a drive during the night.

"Plans changed several times," Orris Rin continued. "It seems that you were not communicating with your friends, but they have somehow been able to track your movements nonetheless. They will not arrive here quickly enough to save you, though. And we've set a little trap for them out here just in case they do show up before we're done with you."

Oliver felt the world start to rotate around him again. That wasn't a good sign at all, he thought. Whether it had been his head cracking on the pavement earlier or the other Kalatari punching him in the face he wasn't sure, but he definitely had a concussion. Or something much, much worse.

"Come on, then. Let's get it done." Orris Rin stopped for a moment to size him up. "You are an idiot, Oliver, but you weren't bad company. This isn't personal."

"Murdering me *feels* pretty personal," Oliver noted.

Orris Rin shrugged. "I suppose so." He nodded at the other Kalatari. "Take him inside." Oliver found himself seized by the arms and propelled rapidly toward the church's front doors.

The interior of the church was more or less what Oliver might have expected. A dozen rows of wooden pews were covered with dust. Stained glass littered the floor, the windows casualties of rock-throwing vandals. The paint on the walls was peeling and the whole place smelled of mildew and rot. Oliver was a little surprised the church hadn't already been torn down. It would have been more trouble to renovate this place than it was probably worth.

What he would have not expected, though, was that the church was full of congregants. About three-quarters of the people inside were ordinary humans. Most of them looked like they'd been roused from their beds to rush here during the night. A few were still in their nightclothes and one man wore shorts with mismatched shoes.

The other quarter of the congregants were Kalatari. Most of them were wearing overcoats or other clothing designed to conceal as much of their bodies as possible. None wore hats as Orris Rin and his compatriot had done outside, but Oliver had no doubt each of them had similarly concealing headgear secreted somewhere within the church.

Several of the Kalatari hissed at him the moment he caught their attention. The humans looked on with expressions ranging from sleepy disinterest to outright fear.

"Behold, the Destroyer!" intoned a woman's voice. Oliver turned to see another Kalatari, arguably a female, standing near the long-disused wooden pulpit. She wore floor-length, silver robes and held a jeweled wooden staff that extended a good two feet above her head.

"You must be the Matriarch," he said.

"Indeed."

Oliver sighed. His head was buzzing now. He could hear

the sound of rushing water, but it was very faint, as if he were hearing a river from a great distance away. "Look, I'm sure we can settle this without anyone getting hurt."

"Silence!" commanded the Matriarch. Orris Rin cuffed Oliver harshly on the back of the head.

"Ow," said Oliver. "Stop that!" Orris Rin blinked in surprise. "Don't hit me again," Oliver said. "I'm getting sick of it."

"Brave," Orris Rin muttered under his breath.

"So, Destroyer, now you have come to stand before me!" the Matriarch intoned gravely.

Oliver had had quite enough of this. "It wasn't my idea!" he said. "I don't know what the hell you're on, but I'm not any Destroyer. I'm an ordinary person. I've been telling your guy here that," he nodded at Orris Rin. "This is all a mistake!"

"You are the enemy of the Kalatari," the Matriarch said.

"I had never heard of the Kalatari until yesterday," Oliver insisted. "I knew nothing about any of you. I still don't." He glared back at Orris Rin. "Get your damn reptile claws off of me! I'm warning you!"

Orris Rin looked amazed at Oliver's boldness. The Matriarch only scowled at him. "You are the Destroyer. I have foreseen this."

"For god's sake," Oliver said. "Why don't you just tell me what it is you foresaw and maybe I can help you work this out?"

"Yes," said a new voice from behind him. "I'd like to hear that as well." Oliver turned his head in surprise. Artemis stood in the back of the church, wearing a black jumper over a light blue blouse. The little girl's arms were crossed sternly in front of her.

Sally Rain and Tyler flanked her on either side. Sally held two curved farmer's sickles, one in each hand. Blood slowly dripped from the blades of each of them. Two pistol holsters were strapped to Sally's upper thighs, and Oliver could see her familiar silver pistols nestled within. She had an evil grin on her face that Oliver found only slightly less disturbing than the fact that she was covered in blood, and none of it appeared to be hers.

Tyler stood next to her in yet another Hawaiian shirt. Oliver wondered if he'd lost the last one to another wolf episode. That had to play hell with a person's wardrobe. *He must buy those shirts in bulk*, Oliver thought.

"*How?*" hissed Orris Rin..

Sally gestured back at the door with one of her sickles. "Your trap?" The two sickles disappeared behind her back in a flurry of motion, only to have her pistols take their places in her hands. "Not so much of a trap," she shrugged dismissively.

"Enough," Artemis told her. She turned her attention to the Matriarch. "Kallas, I am extremely upset with you."

Orris Rin took a step towards the girl, flanked by another of the Kalatari. "You are hopelessly outnumbered," he said to Artemis. He nodded at Oliver. "This man is ours. You have no claim to him. Leave now and you will not be harmed."

"Aw," said Sally. "Do you *promise* not to hurt me?"

"You should thank me," the Kalatari said to her. "For what you have done we should be eating you alive."

Sally took a threatening step toward him but Artemis held up a hand and she stopped in her tracks. "Kallas," Artemis addressed the Matriarch. "You've lost. Free this man and I will forgive your transgressions against me."

"*You* will forgive *us*?" Rin interjected, his tone incredulous. "For what?"

"You assaulted my people and are attempting to murder a man who is under my protection."

"Things we did to defend ourselves," Rin protested. "We have the right to self-preservation."

"What a bunch of crap," Tyler said. "Your boss there ate some bad mushrooms. Screw you. You don't get to kill people because of it."

"I have given a true prophecy," the Matriarch said, pointing at Oliver. "He must die."

"What did you see?" Artemis asked. "What is he?"

The Matriarch paused, eyeing Oliver fearfully. "I was in a holy trance, and Vashka sent a vision to me."

"You dropped acid," Tyler said, rolling his eyes.

"My vision was of that man," she pointed at Oliver again. "He was shown to me, murdering my people. My entire race, wiped out in an instant."

"Bullshit," said Tyler.

"How?" Artemis asked, her eyes intent on the Matriarch. "How did he do it?"

The Matriarch hesitated, looking unsure of how to proceed. "He...erased them," she said. "He erased all of us."

Artemis frowned. "That doesn't make any sense," she said. "Nobody can just..." she trailed off as Jeffrey slipped through the still-open door behind them and strolled casually into the church. The cat rubbed once against Sally's legs, then took a moment to apprise himself of the situation.

"What's going on?" he asked curiously.

Orris Rin and the other Kalatari stared at the cat in stunned silence. Nobody moved. It was one of the humans who finally spoke up, a teenager in a fast food restaurant uniform. "Did that cat just talk?"

"Get used to it," Oliver said. "I did." His head had stopped spinning, but the urge to sleep was getting overwhelming. He knew he wouldn't be able to stay awake for long.

Artemis stared at the cat curiously. "By all the gods," she said suddenly. "It *does* make sense." She turned to Oliver, shock clearly registering on her face. Oliver stared back at her in amazement. It was the first time he had seen a genuine emotional reaction from the girl.

"It makes sense?" Oliver asked.

"It does." Artemis turned to the Matriarch. "Kallas, I have no reason to lie to you. Please believe this. You have one chance to live. You have to let this man go. *Right now*. If you don't, you will be responsible for what happens next. I won't be able to help you."

"The man dies," the Matriarch said firmly.

Artemis sighed softly. "Then I'm sorry." She shrugged. "I'm so sorry. There's nothing I can do for you now."

"Um..." Tyler began. "I think I missed something?"

191

"What's going on?" Oliver asked. "I think you were about to rescue me?"

"No," Artemis said. "I'm not."

"We're not?" Sally asked.

"Wait a damn minute…" Tyler started.

"We don't need to rescue him. Kallas's vision was correct. Mr. Jones *is* the Destroyer."

Tyler stared at her. "You're serious?"

"I am," the little girl said. "He *is* going to kill them all, and there is nothing any of us can do to stop it."

Chapter 21

"I am?" asked Oliver.

"He is?" asked Jeffrey.

"*Really*?" asked Orris Rin suspiciously. "You're sure?" He glanced back at the Matriarch. "I mean, of course the Matriarch is always correct, but...*him*?"

Artemis kneeled down to scratch Jeffrey behind the ears. The cat purred enthusiastically. "He is. As improbable as it may seem, here is the proof. Hello, Jeffrey."

"Hello, Artemis," the cat replied.

Artemis stood and faced Oliver. "You made a cat talk."

"So he did do it! He put the whammy on me!" Jeffrey exclaimed.

"Yes," said Artemis. "He did." She frowned. "I would probably phrase it differently."

"What does that prove?" Tyler asked. "He...*is* a sorcerer? Is that even a thing?"

"He's not a sorcerer," Artemis said. "If he were a sorcerer I'd know what to do with him." She sighed deeply. "If you can't be turned from this path, Kallas, then I will leave you now. You'll forgive me if I don't want to watch another genocide." She shot a disapproving look at Sally Rain. "I've seen quite enough of that." With that said, the girl turned on her heel and started out of the church. "Come along, you two."

Sally and Tyler looked at each other nervously, then back to Artemis. "We can't just leave," Tyler said. "They're going to kill him!"

"No," Artemis said, without looking back. "They were never going to kill him."

"But…"

"Now!" Artemis commanded. It was a tone that did not brook argument. She disappeared through the front door, Sally following a step behind her. Tyler looked at Oliver helplessly, and then followed them out.

"That's it?" Oliver called out after them in disbelief. "That's great, thanks. Thanks a lot."

Jeffrey had stayed behind and now looked at Oliver knowingly. "See? You did put the whammy on me!"

"Stop saying *whammy*," Oliver told him. "That doesn't even mean what you think it means."

Orris Rin glanced back at the Matriarch, then stepped forward and took a long, searching look at Oliver. He seemed to hesitate for a moment, and then he turned and walked silently out the front door after Artemis and the others.

"Chief Minister!" the Matriarch shouted after him. There was no response. Orris Rin was gone.

"I think he just quit," Jeffrey said.

The teenager in the fast food uniform looked at the Matriarch guiltily, then headed for the door as well. Two more humans and another Kalatari followed him. A quiet moment passed, then three more did the same. The Matriarch's followers were deserting her.

"I think they also quit," Jeffrey noted. "Anybody else?" he asked the others. "You better go now, before boss man here puts the whammy on you!"

"Stop saying *whammy*," Oliver repeated. Jeffrey flashed his teeth at Oliver. Was the cat actually grinning at him?

"So now what?" Oliver asked the Matriarch. "Tell you what, how about I walk out of here and none of us ever mentions this again? It's not like anyone would believe I met a bunch of lizard people anyway."

The Matriarch glared at him. "Kalatari," she said.

"I don't care what you're called."

The Matriarch pointed a long, clawed finger at him. "Seize him."

Two of the remaining Kalatari sprang forward and grabbed Oliver by the arms. "Bring him to me!" the Matriarch commanded.

"Oh, this is not good," Jeffrey said. "Hey! I know what would help!"

"What?" Oliver asked. He tried to shake free of the two Kalatari but he couldn't break their grip on him, and moving too quickly made his head spin.

"You know what," said Jeffrey.

"Tell me!" Oliver shouted. He saw the Matriarch draw a long dagger from within her robes. This was it. His friends had abandoned him and these lizard people were going to kill him, right here in this church. What a ridiculous way to die.

"You don't like me to say it," said Jeffrey.

Oliver tried to plant his feet to stop his movement toward the Matriarch and her knife, but he was quickly pulled off balance. One of the Kalatari backhanded him hard across the face. Oliver felt the world spin and the sound of rushing water grew louder in his ears. "Say it!" he shouted to the cat.

"I don't want to say it," the cat said.

"Say it!"

"The *whammy*," Jeffrey purred.

"Damn it!" Oliver had held out a dim hope that the cat had come up with something useful to say. He still didn't understand what Artemis had been talking about. He was going to destroy the Kalatari? Nothing could be done to stop him? And the proof of it was in, of all things, a talking cat?

What did that mean? He hadn't done anything to the cat, whatever it kept insisting to the contrary. He had just wanted someone to talk to. That was all. He hadn't rubbed a magic lamp and told a genie his wish. He hadn't said magic words. He wasn't a damn sorcerer. He had no "powers" to speak of, whatever the cat or anyone else might believe.

He was nearly before the Matriarch now. She raised the dagger and ran her tongue down the length of the blade. In a moment she would drive it into his chest, he was sure. Or maybe she was going to cut his throat. Whatever she intended, this was not going to end well for him. If he was going to do something, he had to do it now.

And then he found himself directly in front of the dagger-wielding Kalatari, close enough that he could have leaned forward and kissed her. This was how his life was going to end? Struck down by some crazy lizard queen? Lizard people? Monsters from a storybook?

"Hey, Oliver?" Jeffrey asked.

"What?"

"Who is Pamela Anderson?"

Oliver stared at the cat in shock. That had been in his dream. They had been talking about mass and energy and thought, and Oliver's ridiculous theory that thoughts could affect matter itself. Think about Pamela Anderson, and Pamela Anderson would appear. And maybe he could whip up a nice Siamese for Jeffrey as well.

The cat couldn't possibly know about any of that, though. He had been dreaming. But that meant this was a dream, didn't it? He was *still* dreaming?

No, he thought. Not a dream. He didn't dream. He had to be hallucinating. He'd been hit in the head so many times now he'd lost count. But what if he'd only really been hit once? What was more likely, that any of this was really happening, or that he was lying unconscious in a hospital bed back in San Francisco, and all of this was the deranged fantasy of his damaged brain?

He'd probably had an accident. Hit by a car crossing the street. Fell in his apartment and hit his head. Any of those things made more sense than what he was experiencing now.

None of this is real, he thought. Not the talking cat, not the vampires, not the lizard people, and not that knife the Matriarch was threatening him with now. It was all a delusion. He needed to wake up; to snap out of this state he was in. It was time to go back to the real world, to go back to his life.

"You are the Destroyer," the Matriarch intoned, raising the dagger high. "Now you will die, and we will endure for ten thousand years."

"Go fuck yourself," said Oliver. "Lizard people," he scoffed. "You aren't real."

The Matriarch faltered, her expression looking as if she had just been slapped across the face. "What did you say?"

Oliver finally shook off the two Kalatari that had been holding his arms fast, but he no longer had the urge to run. He didn't want to go to sleep anymore, either. He wanted to wake up. He felt the world start to rotate once more. The sound of rushing water was nearly upon him now. That had to mean something. "You people," he said. Oliver's vision went blurry for a split second, then snapped back into focus. He shook his head.

"What was that?" Jeffrey asked from behind him. He sounded worried. What had the cat seen?

"Talking lizards," Oliver said. His vision blurred again. Was he waking up? The rushing water sounded all around him. Was this madness about to end? He was going to have quite a story to tell the doctors.

Oliver's vision focused and he stared the Kalatari Matriarch in the eye. "None of you are real," he said.

Oliver heard the rushing water in his ears grow into a thunderous sound, a tsunami that threatened to overtake him and wash everyone away. The world spun faster. Whatever was happening was upon him now. Oliver shut his eyes.

And nothing happened. The sound of the rushing water stopped abruptly and only silence remained. After a short moment Oliver opened his eyes, daring to hope that he would find himself waking up in a hospital. But he was still in the old church. One thing was different, though. The Matriarch and her knife were gone.

"Holy. Shit," said Jeffrey.

Oliver looked back at the cat, and then around the church in surprise. It wasn't just the Matriarch who was missing. *All* of the Kalatari were gone. Only the humans remained, looking around in shock and surprise that mirrored Oliver's own. The church was deathly silent for a moment, and then one of the men began to cry.

"What happened?" Oliver asked.

Artemis reappeared at the door. She looked around the room sadly, and then let out a deep sigh.

"What happened, Mr. Jones?" she asked. "What happened is you just annihilated the entire Kalatari race."

"Oh," said Oliver. He looked around. "So…this is real? I'm not hallucinating?"

"No," the girl said. "You are not."

"I see," Oliver said. And then he promptly fainted.

Chapter 22

This time, Oliver did not dream. He found that his mind was aware of the fact that he was asleep, and he had a sensation of floating. It was as if he were lying on a mattress suspended among the clouds, drifting gently along in the wind. But he saw no images and had no conversations with old college professors or cats. It was a welcome relief.

After a time he felt warmth and realized that it was sunlight on his face. He opened his eyes and found himself in bed in a familiar room. He was back in the time-house he had woken up in earlier, after Sally Rain had drugged him the day this had all begun. Sunlight was streaming through the window, with the Golden Gate Bridge a welcome sight in the distance. He was home again. San Francisco. But how long had he been here?

Tyler was sitting in a chair beside the bed, reading an issue of *Cat Fancy* magazine. He was engrossed enough in it to not notice Oliver had woken.

"Really?" Oliver asked, sitting up.

Tyler looked up. "What?" Oliver nodded at the magazine. "I like cats," Tyler said defensively. "They just don't like me. Not anymore, anyway."

"I just figured you'd be into *Canine Monthly* or something. Checking out the centerfolds."

"There's no such thing as *Canine Monthly*," Tyler protested. "And I'm a werewolf, not some kind of pervert. Do you actually think..." he trailed off, looking at Oliver suspiciously. "You're just messing with me, aren't you?"

"Yes."

"Good," Tyler said. "I guess you're feeling better."

"How long was I asleep?"

"Five days," Tyler said.

"Five days?" Oliver asked, stunned. He looked around the room. "And you brought me here instead of to the hospital?"

Tyler shrugged. "Artemis said there was no need; you were just exhausted. She said the energy required to do...what you did...would have been beyond anything we could comprehend. Rest was the only thing that would help you."

Oliver rubbed his eyes. He wasn't sure he wanted to remember what had happened. "What I did," he mused. "What did I do?"

"The Kalatari are gone," Tyler said.

"But it's more than that," Oliver remembered. "It's not just the ones from the church, is it? Not just the ones who attacked me?"

Tyler shook his head. "No. It's all of them. Everywhere.

Artemis and Seven are still working on it, but as near as we can tell, their entire race was just…wiped off the face of the Earth."

Oliver had no idea how to react to that. It had never been his intention to hurt anyone. He had just wanted to get away and go home, back to his normal life. "All of them?" he repeated quietly.

Tyler nodded. "Yeah. I'm sorry, Oliver. I know that wasn't what you wanted."

Oliver leaned back in the bed and rested his head against the headboard. "I'm a murderer, then."

"Nah," said Sally, entering the room. She was holding a plastic cafeteria tray with three steaming mugs of coffee on it. Jeffrey was at her feet, looking up at Oliver curiously. "Technically, the word you're looking for is *genocide*," she continued. "You're a genocide, not a murderer."

"Sally…" Tyler warned.

Jeffrey jumped up on the bed. "How you doing, boss?" he asked.

Oliver took a mug and stared at the black liquid inside it. He sighed. "I'm a genocide," he said to Jeffrey.

"Oh!" said Jeffrey. "Okay. Hey, did you know nobody can see this house from the outside? I didn't even know it was here until I followed these guys inside. I wanted to order Thai food but they said the delivery guy wouldn't be able to find the address. Or he might show up in the wrong year." He looked at Oliver in confusion. "Your friends are really weird."

"Keep talking, little cat," Sally warned.

"Anyway, it's all over now," Tyler said. "The Kalatari are gone. You're back to normal, more or less. You have to forget about it and move on."

"Forget about it?" Oliver asked. "How am I supposed to forget about something like this? It's insane. All of this is just...madness."

"There are ways," Sally murmured, sipping her coffee.

Tyler glared at her. "Could you attempt to be supportive here?"

Sally shrugged. "Bad shit happens. We've all done things we wish we hadn't. Get over it or kill yourself."

Tyler and Oliver stared at her in surprise. "That was being supportive?" Tyler asked.

"Sure," she shrugged. She sipped her coffee and looked from Tyler to Oliver. "What?"

Oliver looked out the window again. It was a nice day. Maybe he'd go for a walk later and get a little air. It had been a while since he'd been able to do that without looking over his shoulder. As far as he knew, nobody else out there was trying to kill him. He should be safe now, shouldn't he?

He scratched Jeffrey absent-mindedly. And what was he going to do about the cat? Take him home?

"Am I supposed to go home now?" he asked Tyler.

Tyler glanced at Sally, concern flashing across his face. Sally shook her head. "Not yet. Artemis has asked to see you first."

"What for?" Oliver asked.

"Debriefing."

"Debriefing? What am I, a spy?"

"You've had quite an experience," Tyler said reassuringly. "She just wants to talk to you and see that you're all right. Talk about what you're going to do next, and, you know, what you should say to people about where you've been all this time. We'd hardly be civilized if we just kicked you into the street after what you've been through."

Jeffrey nudged Oliver's arm with his nose. "I don't trust the dog," he whispered.

"I'm not a dog," Tyler said.

"You see?" Jeffrey asked. "He heard me with his dog hearing!"

"We all heard you," Sally said. "You don't whisper very well."

Oliver thought about it. He liked Tyler, but he didn't believe him, either. "She's not really *asking* me to come, is she?"

Sally smirked. "Artemis never *asks* anything."

Tyler looked apologetic. "It's not a demand, but..."

"It's like when the Mafia asks you to do something? An offer you can't refuse?"

"Yeah."

"What if I do refuse?"

Sally smiled at him. "Then I'm going to hit you," she said sweetly.

Oliver nearly pointed out that she had already hit him, right here in this room, and it hadn't gone quite as she had planned.

But he thought the better of it. There was no reason to start another fight. Besides, if he was sure of anything, it was that a meeting with Artemis would be inevitable. "I guess I should go say hello, then," he said.

"Aw," Sally pouted. "You sure you want to go peacefully?"

"Yes."

"Well, truth be told, I'm starting to like you," Sally said. "So I wouldn't have hit you very hard."

"Do you ever solve problems without violence?" Oliver asked.

"No," Tyler said under his breath.

"What would the point of that be?" she asked. She looked genuinely confused.

"Forget it," Oliver said. "Let's get going."

"Can I come?" asked Jeffrey.

"Why not?" asked Oliver.

"We're taking the cat?" Sally asked.

"We can hardly leave him here," Tyler pointed out.

Sally shrugged. "He rides with you."

Chapter 23

Sally said goodbye outside the time-house and drove away in her Miata. Tyler and Oliver left in Tyler's Charger. Jeffrey stood up on Oliver's lap, his front paws pressed against the glass so he could look out the window. "This is amazing," he said, watching as they passed by other cars. "I don't know how you people take this for granted."

"We've been in cars before," Oliver said. "So have you, for that matter."

"I know, but it's still amazing."

"You get used to it," Tyler said.

"You can get used to lots of things," Oliver said. "Talking cats, for instance."

Jeffrey looked up at Oliver. "Yeah, I've been meaning to talk to you about that."

"I don't know what I did to you or how to put you back," Oliver said.

"Oh, that's okay," Jeffrey said. "I didn't like it at first, but now I do."

"Really?"

"It comes in handy. I saw a guy eating a sandwich the other day and I said, 'Hey, man, you better drop that sandwich!' And he did! He dropped it and ran away!"

"Oh." Oliver made a mental note to discuss socially appropriate behavior with the cat at some point in the very near future.

"It was a good sandwich," Jeffrey noted. "Talking is good. And there's the other stuff…"

Oliver frowned. "What other stuff? What else have you done?"

"Oh, it's nothing bad," the cat said. "I'm not sure how to explain it. It's my brain."

"Your brain?"

"I didn't *think* like this before," the cat explained. "I mean, I had thoughts, but I didn't think. Not really. And I didn't know things the way I do now. Or as many things. It was like I read the entire encyclopedia all at once, before I even knew what an encyclopedia was. Maybe that doesn't make any sense."

"It makes sense," Oliver said.

Tyler glanced over at him. "It does?"

"Sure," Oliver said. "I wanted you to be able to talk," he said to the cat. "But what would the point of that have been, if you'd had nothing to say?"

"I don't get it," said Jeffrey.

"What would you have said if you could have talked two weeks ago? If suddenly you had the ability to talk, but nothing else had changed?"

"I'd have said, 'Whoa, this is really weird!'"

Tyler laughed. "No, you'd have said, 'eat, eat, eat, pee.'"

"More or less," Oliver said. "It wasn't enough that you gained the ability to speak. That wouldn't have done much of anything, really. In order to talk, to make conversation, a lot more about you had to change. In a way, you aren't a cat at all, not anymore. You're something unique."

"Eat, eat, lick balls, sleep," Tyler continued.

Jeffrey thought it over. "Screw you guys," he said finally.

The cat went back to looking out the window. After a while Tyler said, "Hey, Oliver."

"Yeah?"

"We had some fun, didn't we?"

"Did we?" Oliver asked. Assassination attempts, vampires, and lizard people didn't seem all that fun to him.

"Kind of, right?" Tyler asked. It seemed important to him. In a strange way, Oliver thought, it sounded like Tyler was trying to say goodbye.

"I guess we did," Oliver admitted. "It's certainly been quite an experience."

"Try to remember that," Tyler said. Then he turned on the stereo and Hawaiian music came over the speakers. Oliver kept expecting him to say something else, but he was silent.

They were driving east toward the Financial District. Oliver wondered which building their "base" was in. He expected they operated out of some kind of mysterious underground lair, like the Batcave, maybe. Or maybe the penthouse floor of a skyscraper downtown, someplace that overlooked the entire city and had a helipad so they could rush off to…wherever…at a moment's notice. Oliver was sure that whatever it was would be impressive.

Instead Tyler turned the car into Chinatown and pulled up in front of a run-down restaurant called "Sang Min's Double Happiness." Oliver looked at the sign skeptically. "Are we stopping for lunch first? You sure you want to eat here?"

"We're not eating," Tyler said. "This is the last stop. Come on." He got out of the car and waited for Oliver on the sidewalk.

Jeffrey was still seated in Oliver's lap. "Why don't you wait out here?" Oliver suggested.

"Why? I could eat. I'll get me a little *dim sum*, a little rice…"

"I'm not sure what's going to happen now," Oliver said slowly. "But I'm not sure I'm ever coming out of there."

Jeffrey gave him a worried look. "Then why go in at all?" the cat asked, putting a paw on Oliver's chest and looking him in the eye. "Hit that fool dog in the head and let's get out of here."

Oliver shook his head. "I'm going to see this through," he said.

"Why?"

"Because I've been running for days and I don't want to live like that. And honestly, I don't know what else to do."

Oliver stepped out of the car and placed Jeffrey carefully on the sidewalk, stroking the cat once along the back before following Tyler into the restaurant. He had thought the place might be abandoned, but there were a few people dining inside, and a waiter was taking a tourist couple's order a few feet away. Nobody was acting as if anything were amiss.

Artemis was seated alone in a distant corner booth. She raised a hand and motioned Oliver over. Today she was wearing blue jeans and a t-shirt with a cartoon monster on the front. Oliver was sure he had seen it before, from a children's television show. "Pikachu?" he said as he reached the booth.

"Yes. You seem surprised."

"I'm just surprised you like Pikachu," he said. "Seems like kid stuff, and one thing I'm sure of is that you're not a kid."

"Everyone likes Pikachu," she said matter-of-factly. "Have a seat."

Oliver turned but Tyler wasn't joining them. He'd taken a seat on the other side of the restaurant and was speaking to the waiter. No doubt ordering five or six courses, Oliver thought. As an appetizer. Oliver sat down.

"So this is your secret base?" he asked the girl.

"No," she said. "This is a restaurant I like."

"Oh."

"Is this what you imagined a 'secret base' would look like?"

"No. Not really."

"Well, then." There was no food on the table, but there was a teapot and two small handle-less cups. She poured tea into one for Oliver, then refilled her own. She took a sip of hers and sighed contentedly. "That is *very* good," she said. "It's hard to find good tea."

"Tea all tastes the same to me," Oliver said. She stared at him disapprovingly. "I guess I just haven't tried enough," he offered.

"It doesn't matter now," she said. "So. How are you?"

"Fine, thanks. How are you?"

"No," she said firmly.

"No?"

"I have no tradition of small talk, Mr. Jones," she said. "When I ask you how you are, it is because I am interested in the answer. So once again, how are you?"

Oliver shrugged. "I'm tired. Even though I slept for as long as I did, days I guess, I'm still tired. I'm still confused about all of this, but not like before. I feel this...I don't know...*resignation*. Is that the right word?"

"No," she said. "The word you are looking for is *depression*."

"Oh." He considered that as he took a sip of the tea. "Yeah, you're right."

"Your exhaustion is entirely natural, as such things go, given the amount of energy you expended without any practice."

"Practice?"

"Rather like if you decided to take up jogging, and on your first day out ran a marathon. It's a lucky thing the stress didn't kill you."

"I feel like you're telling me how the story ends and

skipping the beginning," Oliver said.

"Oh?"

Oliver looked the little girl in the eyes. "How did I do it? What am I?"

"Oh, I see," Artemis said. She took another sip of her tea. "It took me a while to put that all together. Too long, really, but in my defense it is an exceptionally rare thing. And the truth is, I don't know. Not exactly. In a manner of speaking, I can tell you the symptom, but not the disease."

Oliver sighed. He had been hoping he was finally going to get some answers, but that was looking less likely now. "All right, then. What's the symptom?"

"You change reality," the girl said simply.

"I..." he stared at her. "Change reality? Are you making a joke?"

"Do I strike you as someone who makes jokes?"

"No."

"Then it is not very likely that I began doing so just now, is it?"

Oliver opened his mouth, shut it, then opened it again. "I'm going to need a little more than that," he said.

"I have little more. I have only heard stories about it, back when I was very young. You have the power, or perhaps I should say the ability, to alter reality. Using only this," she said, tapping her index finger against her temple.

"That's obviously not true," Oliver said. "If I could change the world at will I'd...I'd be rich, for one thing. And taller."

"You certainly would, if you had any control over it."

"Excuse me?"

"It's clear to me that everything you are capable of doing occurs on an almost entirely subconscious level. You didn't will for any of the strange things that have happened to happen, did you? Did you say, 'Oh, poor me. I'm so lonely, I wish my cat could talk.'"

Oliver considered making a rude remark, but decided against it. "No."

"No, you did not. You wanted a companion, and suddenly your cat spoke to you. Did you wish for the Kalatari to be wiped out of existence?"

"No."

"What did happen?"

The memories were hazy, but Oliver knew the answer. "I'd been hit in the head so many times I couldn't control my mind anymore," he said. "I thought I was hallucinating. I thought I must have brain damage and that everything that was happening was a fantasy."

"And?"

"I convinced myself that none of it was real. That it *wasn't* happening. Lizard people *aren't* real," he said.

"And as such, they are no longer real," Artemis said. "There are none left."

"Yeah."

"You may have committed genocide, Mr. Jones, but it would be fair to say that you did it by accident. I think without

213

the drugs and head trauma, you could never have pulled it off. Perhaps that will help you to sleep at night."

Oliver blinked. "That's supposed to help?"

"Why not?" the girl shrugged. "I myself was surprised to learn that the Matriarch did indeed have the gift of prophecy. Of course, it was that same prophecy that led directly to her ruin. If the Kalatari had left you alone, they'd all be alive today. Or at least until their natural extinction, which wasn't far off anyway."

John Blackwell had given the Kalatari another hundred years, Oliver remembered. "But doesn't all of that make me…"

"Unbelievably dangerous?" the girl asked.

"Yeah."

"Yes, it does," Artemis said. "You may be the single most dangerous person on this planet."

"Oh."

"And not in the least to yourself. You willed the Kalatari out of existence, albeit unwittingly. What is to say that you couldn't do the same thing to yourself?"

"You can *do* that?"

"I can't," Artemis said. "You could."

The waitress appeared with a fresh pot of tea, whisking the old one away. Oliver wondered if food was coming. He wasn't sure how long it had been since he'd eaten. Had they fed him intravenously while he had slept? He hadn't noticed any equipment for that in the room.

"So," Artemis said. "What are we going to do with you?"

"Do with me?"

"I suppose you could return to your life," Artemis said. "Go back to your house. We cleaned it up for you. Got rid of the bodies and fixed your window, even. You could go back to work tomorrow."

"How am I going to pull that off?" Oliver asked. "The last time I was at my office…"

"It would take me exactly one phone call," Artemis said. She looked directly at him. "Do you really doubt I could do this?"

"No," Oliver said.

"So then. Back to your old life. You'll have Jeffrey, of course. He seems attached to you. But everything else will be just like it was. You'll work on those spreadsheets of yours all day and then go home to eat Lean Cuisine."

"I don't eat Lean Cuisine," Oliver lied.

"Of course you don't," Artemis said. She sighed. "But it does occur to me that perhaps you'd like to do something more with your life."

"Such as?"

"Well, you're smart. You're capable. You have some experience now with the paranormal. For that matter you *are* the paranormal, and you've dealt with rapid changes in your life fairly well. A man with a lesser mind would have required institutionalization by now."

"Thanks." Oliver still wasn't entirely convinced that he wasn't really lying unconscious in a bed somewhere, while all of this around him was a fantasy.

"What I'm saying is that I could find a place for you on my team. I think you would be an asset."

Oliver blinked. "You're offering me a job?" he asked.

"I thought I had made that clear," Artemis said.

"But...even though I can't..." Oliver wiggled his fingers in the air. "Go 'woo woo' and make things appear?" He wondered what good he could possibly be to her.

Artemis rolled her eyes. "Yes, Mr. Jones, in spite of the fact that you can't go 'woo woo,' I'd like you to join us."

Oliver considered it. This was all moving very fast. "Can I have a few days to think about it?"

"No," Artemis said. "You already have all the information you need to decide right now. Either I'm going to find a desk for you back at our 'secret base,' or I'll thank you for your time and Tyler will drive you home, never to see any of us again."

Oliver opened his mouth, intending to refuse, but then he caught himself. Just a few days ago he'd been lamenting about how dull his life was. Then all of this craziness had happened. He'd been chased by an assassin. Drank wine with a vampire. Been bitten by another vampire. And he'd annihilated an entire species of lizard people, although in his defense they had been trying to murder him at the time.

Life didn't have to be dull. There was so much more out there in the world, and he had to admit, he wanted to see more of it.

"I'm in," Oliver said.

"Oh, thank god," Tyler said from behind him. Oliver turned his head. Tyler had crossed to their side of the restaurant unseen, and was standing adjacent to the booth just behind them. More disconcerting was the sight of Sally Rain, who had seemingly appeared from nowhere and was now standing directly behind Oliver. She held a sinister-looking syringe in her hand, pointed directly at his neck.

Sally capped the syringe and put it in her jacket pocket with god knew whatever else she kept in there. "Welcome aboard," she said.

"Great job, buddy," Tyler said.

Oliver turned back to Artemis, full of shock and anger. "What was that?" he asked. "You were going to kill me if I said no?"

"No," she said, her face impassive. "It would be too dangerous to kill you. I'm not sure what would happen if I tried."

"What was that about, then?"

"Quarantine," the girl said. "You would have woken up somewhere far away from here, where you wouldn't be a danger to anyone."

"Why?" Oliver asked.

"Mr. Jones, do you really think I can have you running around out in the world unsupervised? Knowing the things you can do? I would turn you loose on this world no sooner than I would provide an infant access to a nuclear weapon." She thought about what she had just said for a moment. "Although I suppose in that analogy, you are both the infant *and* the weapon."

"But you could have just said that, instead of pretending to give me a choice!" Oliver protested.

"You did have a choice," she shrugged. "We are none of us slaves, Oliver. You had to choose to be one of us freely, without conditions attached. And now you've made that choice. Congratulations are in order, I suppose. Are you sure you won't have some tea?"

"You're crazy," Oliver said. He looked back at Tyler and Sally. "You're all crazy!"

"You really have no idea," Sally smirked.

Oliver heard a commotion at the restaurant's door and turned to look. A thin man with short, wildly uncombed hair and round eyeglasses was hurtling toward their table, carrying what looked like an iPad. From his twitchy, nervous demeanor, Oliver guessed he was an aficionado of strong coffee, or quite possibly much more serious stimulants.

"Oh, good," Tyler said. "You can finally meet Seven." He turned to the approaching man. "Seven, this is…"

Seven brushed past him. "Not now," he said, thrusting the tablet computer he carried toward Artemis. "You are not going to believe this," he said.

Artemis studied the screen for a moment, her expression never changing. "My goodness," she said. "That is quite a problem, isn't it?"

"What is?" Sally asked, coming around to look.

"Mr. Jones, I hope you don't mind, but time is a factor now," Artemis said. "We will have to discuss your salary requirements and conduct your orientation later."

"You do an orientation?" he asked.

"Of course we do," she said. "Do you think we just send

218

people out into the field without any training?" Tyler glanced at her skeptically. "Don't answer that," she continued. "Tyler, we're going to need some candy."

"You want me to run to 7-11?" Tyler asked in disbelief. "Now?"

"Not that kind of candy," Artemis said. "What we need is in the Vault."

"Oh," Tyler said. "Oh wow."

"Indeed." She stood up. "Come along, Mr. Jones. We'll have to explain things to you on the way." She headed for the door.

Oliver hesitated for a moment, and then turned to follow her. He wasn't sure what this new life was going to be like, but he was certain it would never be dull. He was living in interesting times, like the old Chinese saying went. Time would only tell whether that was a good thing or a bad thing. "May you live in interesting times" was a curse, after all.

Three hours later, when he saw the dragon for the first time, Oliver had his answer.

ABOUT THE AUTHOR

Matthew Storm lives above a bar in Tokyo, where he is occasionally visited by a stray cat who may or may not speak.

Matthew is on Twitter: @mjstorm

58789930R00126

Made in the USA
Lexington, KY
17 December 2016